"Open your eyes, Phoenix," Deborah said nudging his shoulder.

"Why?" he growled

quest.

"Come on," she c...
enough for me to che...
fected by the concussi...
sleep."

Even though his eyes remained closed, he reached out with both hands and clamped his hands around her waist. "We've been doing things your way all night. Now we'll try them my way." He lifted her easily over him and rolled over to face her when she was lying next to him. Ignoring her soft protest, he tucked her against him, then buried his face in the fragrant curve of her throat.

Deborah was shocked to discover one of her hands was clenching his shoulder. Holding on, not pushing him away. "Phoenix, let me up."

His reply was muffled against her throat. "No."

He'd thrown one of his legs over hers, anchoring her firmly into the mattress. She should be outraged. She should be yelling at him. She should be threatening him with bodily harm. She wasn't doing any of those things.

Rather than ask herself why she wasn't angry, she slid her fingers over the corded muscles of his shoulder under his open shirt and let them feather through his thick hair. When he made a soft sound of pleasure, she did it again.

It wasn't exactly how the test should be done, but she decided to improvise. "Phoenix, what's my name?"

"Flame," he murmured. "Fire Woman with hair the color of hot coals."

Was he rambling in his sleep or hallucinating? She didn't know. "Phoenix, does your head still ache?"

"I ache," he said huskily. "But not my head . . ."

WHAT ARE *LOVESWEPT* ROMANCES?

They are stories of true romance and touching emotion. We believe those two very important ingredients are constants in our highly sensual and very believable stories in the *LOVESWEPT* line. Our goal is to give you, the reader, stories of consistently high quality that may sometimes make you laugh, sometimes make you cry, but are always fresh and creative and contain many delightful surprises within their pages.

Most romance fans read an enormous number of books. Those they truly love, they keep. Others may be traded with friends and soon forgotten. We hope that each *LOVESWEPT* romance will be a treasure—a "keeper." We will always try to publish

LOVE STORIES YOU'LL NEVER FORGET
BY AUTHORS YOU'LL ALWAYS REMEMBER

The Editors

Patt Bucheister
Mischief and Magic

BANTAM BOOKS
NEW YORK · TORONTO · LONDON · SYDNEY · AUCKLAND

MISCHIEF AND MAGIC

A Bantam Book / September 1992

If you would be interested in receiving protective vinyl
covers for your Loveswept books, please write to this address
for information:

Loveswept
Bantam Books
P.O. Box 985
Hicksville, NY 11802

ISBN 0-553-44079-9

Published simultaneously in the United States and Canada

Bantam Books are published by Bantam Books, a division of
Bantam Doubleday Dell Publishing Group, Inc. Its trademark,
consisting of the words "Bantam Books" and the portrayal of
a rooster, is Registered in U.S. Patent and Trademark Office
and in other countries. Marca Registrada. Bantam Books, 666
Fifth Avenue, New York, New York 10103.

PRINTED IN THE UNITED STATES OF AMERICA

OPM   0 9 8 7 6 5 4 3 2 1

To Albert and Suzanne Elrod
for their humor, their affection,
and their long-suffering friendship.
May your lives always be filled with orchids in bloom.

One

Phoenix Sierra was going to fire his secretary. She probably wouldn't take him seriously since she was fired on a fairly regular basis, but this time he meant it. Belle was going to get her walking papers.

Just as soon as he got out of the emergency room.

Phoenix liked to think he was as good a sport as the next guy, but Belle had gone too far with her idea of a prank. Few people understood the intricacies of a well-done practical joke, he theorized. Even fewer appreciated being on the receiving end. At the moment he was one of them. As much as he had to admire his secretary's ingenuity, he didn't think her attempt was particularly funny. Painful, but not funny.

"A chicken," he muttered disgustedly. A live blood-thirsty chicken had attacked him, and he was going to fire Belle.

It didn't matter that Belle was the only one who could find anything in the office. Though to be honest, if it weren't for Belle's screwy but efficient system of bookkeeping, he and his brother, Denver, would still be building and renovating houses in the Richmond, Virginia, area, but they wouldn't have any records to show they were getting paid for it. But just because Belle had worked for him and Denver ever since they'd started the Sierra Construction Company didn't mean she could get away with murder.

Murder, he thought wistfully, looking down at his right arm, which was wrapped in a gauzy towel. It was really too bad murder was against the law. Even if there wasn't any concrete proof that Belle had put the vicious chicken in his car, she was the only one—other than his brother—who'd threatened lately to pay him back for a practical joke he'd pulled. Since Denver and his wife, Courtney, were out of town for the weekend, and since Belle had known about his plans for the evening and that he would be taking his Porsche instead of his truck, she was the only person who had motive, means, and opportunity. He didn't need to be a licensed private investigator to figure out she was the guilty party.

Fighting impatience, Phoenix adjusted the absorbant towel that had partially fallen off his forearm. The nurse who had settled him on the examination table fifteen minutes earlier had wrapped the towel around the worst of his wounds, then had left a stack of them next to him. Apparently they were to be used as reinforcements while he waited to be seen by a doctor. She'd obviously known it would be a while. He hadn't had a glimpse of the nurse or anyone else since he'd been parked in the curtained cubicle.

He looked down at the numerous nicks and cuts on his arm, as well as the previously stitched injury that was about an inch away from one of the slashes made by one of the chicken's claws. Two visits to the emergency room in one week was a bit much, he mused. This certainly seemed to be his week for accidents, except that this one wasn't an accident exactly. Whatever he wanted to call it, it was going to be hard to explain. Cutting his arm while at a construction site was fairly routine. Being attacked by a chicken wasn't.

It was probably too much to hope he'd get a different doctor from the one who'd treated him after his run-in with the goat his brother had put in his apartment. Phoenix had tried to explain to the doctor how the goat had been a practical joke that had backfired, but he could tell the honorable physician hadn't understood the finer points of his type of humor. Describing the incident with the chicken wasn't going to be any easier.

He glanced down at his narrow pleated dress shirt and tuxedo slacks. He might not have the worst injury in the emergency room, but he would bet he was the best-dressed walking wounded there. The ends of his black formal tie hung down on either side of his unbuttoned dress shirt. He'd made that adjustment to his attire so the nurse could make sure his heart was still beating.

He grimaced as he thought about his tuxedo jacket, which he'd wrapped around the squirming chicken in order to get it out of his car and into the SPCA office. At the time he hadn't stopped to consider what a chicken with a pointed beak, razor-sharp talons, and poor personal hygiene could do to a rented tuxedo jacket. The jacket was the first thing he'd thought of to use. Perhaps if he hadn't removed it, it would have protected his arm better, but all he'd wanted to do was control the chicken long enough to evict it from his car.

He sighed heavily. This was not the way he'd planned to spend Saturday night. Instead of it being his first date with the attractive Stacy McGillis, it was his last date with her. She hadn't been at all amused when he'd called her from his car as he drove himself to the hospital. Nor had she taken it well when he'd told her he wouldn't be able to take her to the Autumn Charity Ball that night. He supposed he really couldn't blame her for not accepting his explanation. And if he remembered correctly, the curvaceous blonde had stated emphatically that she didn't intend to go out with him in this lifetime or the next.

The curtain separating his cubicle from the next wavered slightly. He heard a series of shuffling sounds followed by the creaking rattle of wheels. His neighbor was apparently being transferred to parts unknown. It was an encouraging sign that someone was being taken care of, even though he wasn't.

A nurse parted the curtain and poked her head in long enough to say brightly. "Dr. Justin will be with you shortly, Mr. Sierra." She was gone before he could comment, leaving a fluttering curtain in her wake.

He grabbed another towel and wrapped it awkwardly around his arm, making sure the plastic side was protecting his dress slacks. He didn't know why he was bothering. He was going to have to pay for the damages, and that meant buying the entire tuxedo, which consisted of a ruined jacket and shirt and a pair of pants with a stripe down the side that he'd never wear. The only other time he'd worn a tuxedo was when Denver and Courtney were married. There wasn't a woman alive who could make him wear a monkey suit again.

Holding the towel around his arm, he arched his back to ease the stiffness from sitting in one place so long. Earlier the nurse had tried to persuade him to lie down while she took his blood pressure, temperature, and medical history. He had refused. He felt like a big enough idiot as it was. Lying on his back staring at acoustical tile would make him feel even more ridiculous.

Besides, as tired as he was, he might fall asleep if he became horizontal for the first time in over thirty-six hours. He'd spent most of the previous night driving around looking for a sixteen-year-old runaway. When he'd started Friends of the Court to help teenagers in trouble, he hadn't planned on partaking in late-night search-and-rescue missions. Or on feeling so torn up when the system failed or the kids refused to be helped.

He was about one minute away from leaving when the curtain was pulled back, then closed again. Phoenix looked up, expecting to see a nurse, and found himself staring instead at a copper-haired woman who was wearing a white coat and studying a clipboard.

She was stunning. And he was stunned.

At first glance she was the epitome of a professional woman. His second and third glances made him concentrate on the woman beneath the white coat. Gazing at her, he absorbed the impact of instant attraction, of immediate, gut-wrenching desire knotting his stomach.

He hadn't even seen her eyes, for cripes' sake, he thought, and he was practically hyperventilating. If the nurse took his blood pressure now, she would find it elevated, his pulse erratic.

A stethoscope dangled from around her slender neck, the round part nestling in the V of her buttoned white coat. Phoenix caught a glimpse of a tan linen skirt that was too long, preventing him from getting a good view of her legs. Moving his gaze upward, he saw an oblong plastic name tag attached to the coat's upper pocket, but he was too far away to read the small block lettering. As he let his gaze rise to her hair, he wondered how it would look hanging loose instead of confined in the intricately woven French braid. Would it curl softly on her shoulders, or lie lusciously thick, or be like strands of silk when he ran his fingers through it?

When she stepped closer, he caught a hint of jasmine mixed with antiseptic. For some odd reason, he found it a very stimulating combination.

Maybe he'd lost more blood than he thought.

When she looked up from the clipboard, he felt his heart rock uncomfortably as her gaze collided with his. Her eyes were the color of rich brown sugar, he realized, and was surprised at the fanciful thought. He wasn't poetic by nature, but this woman was making his blood sing and his body chime with lyrical vibrations.

"Mr. Sierra?"

Her voice matched the honey color of her eyes, warm and delicious.

He corrected her automatically. "Phoenix."

She consulted the clipboard again. When she brought her gaze back up to his, she was smiling faintly. "And here I thought you'd put your home-town on the wrong line. You aren't *from* Phoenix. You *are* Phoenix. You have a distinctive first name, Mr. Sierra."

He'd heard that before, but never in an evocative voice that made him think of hot satin on a cold night. "It could have been even more distinctive if my mother had her way," he said. "She wanted to call me Tame Wolf."

Tilting her head to one side, she glanced at his injured arm and formal attire. "Maybe Wild Wolf would have been more appropriate. You don't appear to be leading a tame life."

He allowed himself to relax when he saw only amusement in her eyes and no sign of derision about his Indian background.

"Wild Wolf was designated for my brother," he said.

"And what name did he get instead?"

"Denver."

When she pursed her lips in a silent whistle of admiration, he thought he was going to explode.

Then she said, "I'm sorry my parents didn't have the imagination yours did. I'm Dr. Justin."

Holding the towel so it wouldn't fall off, he raised his right arm a few inches. "I'd shake hands, but I'm having a little problem with my arm at the moment."

"So I see. We'll take care of that for you." Again her gaze roamed over his pleated dress shirt and tuxedo slacks. "It must have been quite a party."

"I never made it. This happened in my car."

She raised one eyebrow but didn't make any comment. Her lack of curiosity made him wonder if she just wasn't the curious sort, or if, in her occupation, she'd already heard just about everything there was to hear.

She put the clipboard down beside him on the table and moved closer to examine his injury. Because his arm was resting on his thigh and because he was sitting up, she had to stand between his legs in order to reach his arm.

She raised her eyes to his when he suddenly drew in his breath. "Are you in pain, Mr. Sierra?"

"Not the kind you mean," he said huskily. His gaze lowered to her slender hips. He knew she hadn't intended the position to be intimate, but it felt damn personal to him. "It's my normal reaction," he added, "when I have a beautiful woman between my legs."

She didn't respond. She simply slipped on a pair of surgical gloves and unwrapped the towel from around his arm. "Aha," she murmured profoundly.

"Aha what?"

"Have you had much experience with doctors, Mr. Sierra?"

Instead of answering her question, he asked one of his own. "I don't suppose you would use my first name?"

"No, I don't suppose I would." She reached for a sterile pack the nurse had placed on a tray table beside the examination table. "You haven't answered my question."

"As you can see by the stitches already in my arm, one experience with a doctor was fairly recent. Why do you ask?"

After cleaning his arm with an antiseptic solution, she picked up a hypodermic syringe and held it point up. "One of the things we learn in med school is how to deaden parts of the body."

He smiled. "How comforting."

"It is to the patient, and sometimes to the doctor when certain portions of a patient's anatomy are creating problems."

"I'll remember that," he murmured, keeping a wary glance on the needle in her hand just in case it moved lower than his arm.

"I thought you might." She gently lifted his arm and swabbed a small area. "Think pleasant thoughts for a second, Mr. Sierra. I'm going to give you an injection to deaden the area before I close this cut in your arm."

He didn't feel a thing. He was too busy trying to control his response to having her touch him. Even with the barrier of gloves, he could feel a current of heat on his skin from her hand. Her head was bent as she concentrated on what she was doing, so he looked at her name tag. Dr. Deborah Justin. Deborah, he recited silently. He couldn't recall knowing any other woman with that name. Which was appropriate. He had never met anyone quite like her before. Nor had he ever reacted to any other woman the way he was reacting to her.

Whether she really was interested or was simply making conversation to put him at ease, she said, "The doctor who stitched up your previous injury did a very neat job. I'll try to do the same with this one so you'll have a matched set. Maybe you should think about getting a different car."

She was sharp, he thought. And that was good. He preferred an edge over dullness any day. "The first cut was from a jagged nail sticking out of a board. The board was part of a ceiling that started to come down, and since I was under it at the time, my initial reaction was to try to hold it up."

"Sort of like Atlas holding up the world?"

Damn, but he liked her dry humor. So far he hadn't found an awful lot he didn't like about her. Except she refused to use his first name.

"It felt like it at the time," he said, chuckling.

While waiting for the Xylocaine to take effect, she treated the other smaller wounds. "And these cuts?" she asked.

His gaze fixed on some silken strands of her hair that had come loose and were caressing her cheek. "Would you believe I was attacked by a chicken?"

She didn't even pause. "I need to get out more," she murmured. Lifting his arm to slip another gauze towel under it to protect his slacks, she added, "I didn't realize farmers dressed so formally."

"I'm in construction, not farming. The chicken was in my car."

"Couldn't get a date?"

Phoenix choked suddenly, then laughed so hard, she had to stop what she was doing until he calmed down. Still chuckling, he explained, "The chicken was my secretary's idea of a practical joke. She knew I was going to be in fancy duds and would be using my car instead of the truck tonight. It was a perfect setup for revenge."

Briefly, her eyes met his. She frowned for a few seconds, then her expression altered, and she became the stoic physician once again.

"Did you neglect to give her a raise?" she asked as she picked up a suture needle.

"It wasn't that kind of revenge. She was a little miffed when I put some goldfish in the office water cooler. She said it was the last straw. Three nights later I encountered a chicken in my car."

"Do you do that sort of thing often?"

She'd given him that odd look again, but he'd be damned if he could figure out what emotion had flickered in her eyes. "Putting goldfish in water coolers or running into chickens in automobiles?"

"Either one."

He shrugged and received a disgruntled look from her when he inadvertently moved his arm. "Sorry," he murmured, then returned to the original subject. "I have been known to pull the occasional practical joke or two, but only on people I like."

"A dubious honor."

"Don't you like practical jokes, Deborah?"

Her only reaction to his informal use of her name was a single raised brow. "At one time I thought they were hilarious."

"What changed your mind?"

"I grew up," she said dryly.

"Meaning I haven't?" He didn't know why her

opinion mattered. She was only thinking the same thing many people thought about him, and it was an image he purposely promoted. He could count on one hand the people who understood that about him.

"It's none of my business," she said, "what you do for entertainment, except when you end up in the emergency room when I'm on duty."

He wanted it to be her business. He wanted her to be interested in everything about him, as he was about her. "We could change that easily enough."

She didn't have a chance to answer. A nurse he hadn't seen before yanked back the curtain. "Dr. Justin, the mother of the child with the broken leg wants to know if she can go along with her daughter to X ray."

Keeping her attention on the suture needle and Phoenix's arm, she answered, "I'd rather the mother remained in the waiting room, Sarah. It won't help the little girl to have her hysterical mother going with her. She's already frightened enough. See if Fran is free to take the girl down to X ray."

The nurse grinned. "Granny Franny. Gotcha."

Phoenix waited until the curtain fell in place again, then asked, "Granny Franny?"

"Fran is a grandmother of five and one of our most experienced nurses. She has a magic touch with children."

Speaking of magic, Phoenix mused, he was feeling somewhat spellbound at the moment himself. Her touch was driving him crazy, even though he knew that wasn't her intention. He watched as she tied off the last stitch, admiring her deft, graceful fingers as she applied a sterile gauze dressing and strips of tape over his stitched wound.

"It looks like you're having a busy night," he commented.

"Just the usual Saturday crowd." She looked up at him, smiling. "Although I can honestly say I've never treated a chicken-attack victim before."

"I'm glad I could contribute something to your evening."

His mouth went dry when she held his right hand in hers and began to examine his fingers by sliding the soft pad of her thumb over each one. He caught the puzzled expression in her eyes as she picked up his other hand, then felt a trickle of awareness down his spine when she brushed her thumb over the tiny crisscross scars in his palm.

"I don't want you to think I'm complaining," he said, his voice oddly husky, "but the chicken didn't hurt my hands."

She stroked his palm. "I was curious about these marks on your hands. One of my vices."

"Hands or scars?"

"Curiosity."

"Feel free to satisfy your curiosity on any other part of my anatomy you want," he drawled.

"You're too kind," she said with cool irony. She released his hand and took a pen out of her breast pocket. Stepping over to the tray table, she started to write on his chart. "My nurse will give you instructions on changing the dressing and when you should go to your family doctor to have those stitches removed."

"I want you to take them out."

She kept writing. "I'm not your personal physician, Mr. Sierra."

"You are now."

She looked up. "As familiar as you seem to be with emergency rooms, you should know we only treat the patients who come in on an emergency basis."

He held her gaze, his own serious. "I want to see you again."

She picked up the clipboard and held it in front of her like a shield, her arms crossed over the back of it. "No."

"Just like that? A simple no? Can't we even discuss it—say, over dinner tomorrow night?"

"No, Mr. Sierra," she answered, her voice soft yet firm. "Will you be needing anything for pain?"

"The only pain I seem to be suffering from at the moment is rejection."

She smiled distantly. "I'm sure you'll recover as quickly from your bruised ego as you will from the cut on your arm." She hesitated, then asked, "Would you mind if I give you a little advice, Mr. Sierra?"

He had the feeling he wasn't going to like what she was going to say. "You're the doctor."

"Strictly from a medical standpoint, I suggest you take it easy on the practical jokes. They seem to be backfiring on you. Not everyone appreciates slapstick humor, and the next time you might not be quite so lucky."

Tilting his head to one side, he asked, "What kind of humor do you like, Deborah?"

The only sign he had that she objected to his use of her first name was a glitter of irritation in her amber eyes. He was very pleased to see it. She was too self-contained, and he had a strong desire to stir her up. Hell, he admitted, he had an urgent desire for more than that. He wanted to taste her mouth and discover the feel of the slender body beneath the white coat. It didn't look as if he was going to be able to do either one. Yet.

"I prefer a more subtle humor," she answered.

"Give me an example of subtle humor."

"Cary Grant and Deborah Kerr in *An Affair to Remember.*

"Ah," he murmured. "A romantic."

"Ah," she replied. "A cynic." She replaced her pen in the breast pocket of her starched coat and asked in her professional voice, "Do you have someone to drive you home, Mr. Sierra? I don't advise you using your right arm until the Xylocaine wears off."

"I've been through this routine before, so I had one of the nurses call a friend of mine when I got here." For effect he added, "He's a cop."

She gave him a mock-surprised look, as though she couldn't believe he would be on friendly terms with a policeman instead of being chased by one. "I trust you haven't pulled any of your jokes on your friend. He could have you arrested."

"As a matter of fact, I have, although he isn't aware of it. I introduced him to my secretary, and he's going out with her. I can't think of a more delicious joke than that."

"Your secretary is dating a policeman?" she asked, and her voice cracked a little.

He was puzzled by her reaction but simply said, "It would take a man wearing a gun and carrying handcuffs to handle Belle."

She closed her eyes, and her face was suddenly pale. Phoenix almost hopped off the examination table to go to her, but she opened her eyes again and stared at him with an oddly stricken look.

"Deborah? What's wrong?"

She shook her head and became the in-control doctor again. "Nothing." She started to walk toward the curtain, then stopped and glanced back at him. "I'm sorry about your arm, Mr. Sierra."

"Why?" he asked, baffled by her serious apology. "It isn't your fault."

Her mouth twisted into a rueful smile. "It might be," she said softly.

Phoenix stared at the curtain as it closed behind

her. He wanted to go after her. He wanted to tell her he was going to see her again, and not as patient and doctor. The injection she'd given him hadn't deadened the desire that had him taut and aching. But he stayed where he was, going over the last few minutes, attempting to figure out what she'd meant when she'd implied she was responsible for his injury. That was ridiculous, considering the circumstances, and he couldn't understand why she would say such a thing.

Nor why an odd loneliness had seeped into his chest when she'd disappeared on the other side of the curtain.

He eased his long frame off the table and stepped out of his cubicle. Scanning the emergency room, he saw a number of people bustling around the center counter area, which seemed to be the hub for the medical personnel. A doctor talked on a telephone, a nurse leaned against the counter as she wrote on a medical record, an orderly pushed a metal cart into another cubicle.

There were many people in the emergency room, but none of them was Dr. Deborah Justin.

Phoenix did recognize one person, a tall, slim man wearing a police uniform. He was heading toward the counter, then spotted Phoenix and changed course, crossing the crowded area like a thin oar cleaving through a sea of bodies.

"Now what did you do?" he asked when he reached Phoenix.

Phoenix took exception to his friend's disgusted tone of voice. Stan made it sound as though he did this sort of thing on purpose. "I didn't do anything except try to get a stupid chicken out of my car."

It took a full thirty seconds for the otherwise sharp policeman to respond. "Excuse me?"

"You heard me. A chicken was put in my car by your girlfriend. It attacked me."

"A chicken," Stan murmured, as though repeating the word would make the meaning clearer.

Not bothering to disguise his irritation, Phoenix snapped, "A chicken. You know, feathers, beak, lays eggs and clucks. A chicken. Surely, you've heard about them."

Stan tried to contain his laughter, but he managed for only a few seconds. Using his uninjured arm, Phoenix yanked him into the cubicle. "Damm it, Stan. Do you have to cackle like a drunken rooster?"

His choice of words set Stan off again. Phoenix waited for him to stop. When his friend's laughter died to an occasional chuckle and a wide grin, he asked sourly, "Finished?"

"For now," Stan replied, smiling broadly. "Why would Belle put a chicken in your car?"

"It was her perverted way of getting back at me for putting goldfish in the water cooler."

"Serves you right," Stan said unsympathetically. "I'd probably have done something just as drastic if you pulled any of your stunts on me."

"I wouldn't do that. You wear a gun."

For the first time Stan noticed Phoenix's clothes. "Hot date?"

"Not anymore. For some reason, the woman I was going to wine and dine didn't believe me when I told her why I couldn't take her to the charity ball."

"She must not know you very well. I wasn't a bit surprised when I got the call to come to get you in the emergency room. Are you ready to get out of here? My partner dropped me off. I'll drive your car, and he'll meet me at your apartment."

As he walked outside with Stan, Phoenix was surprised by his reluctance to leave. His arm had been treated, but he had the unsettled feeling he was leaving something important behind. And he knew what it was. Who it was. Dr. Deborah Justin.

A serious professional woman wasn't usually his type, but for some reason that didn't matter. He wanted to see her again. He would see her again. He didn't know when and he didn't know how, but he was definitely going to see her again—if only to ask her why she thought his episode with the chicken was her fault.

She had implied she didn't think much of his sense of humor. That was okay. That was only a small part of who he was, a facade he'd erected years ago. He'd allowed only a few people to see the man behind his self-imposed barrier. Deborah Justin might turn out to be another. He would see her again.

Even if he had to have another run-in with a berserk chicken.

Deborah was finally able to take a break thirty minutes after she'd treated Phoenix Sierra. Sinking down onto the worn couch in the staff lounge, she kicked off her shoes and put her feet up on a low table, edging some of the magazines out of the way. The usual collection of Styrofoam cups was scattered around, but she refused to pick them up this time. The empty cardboard pizza container could stay where it had been abandoned too. Somebody else could clean up the mess for a change.

Leaning back, she closed her eyes, then snapped them open when the vision of a man's chiseled features, dark hair, and penetrating dark gray eyes materialized behind her closed lids. She sighed. She'd always taken such pride in her professionalism, but it had gone on a brief vacation the instant she'd met Phoenix Sierra's penetrating gaze. Usually, she could put her personal feelings aside no matter what the circumstances or medical emergency. It was one of the hardest things she'd had to learn over the years, but she thought she'd mastered the necessary submerging of her emotions. She'd been wrong.

The moment she'd seen Phoenix Sierra, she'd had to struggle against the attraction that sprang up instantly between them. She could tell herself from now until the end of her shift that it was just her imagination, she was overtired, there was a full moon, or any other rationalization, but it wouldn't change the facts.

Nothing she'd studied in medical school or seen as a "carny kid" had prepared her for the primitive stirring in her blood when she'd touched Phoenix Sierra. The closest she could come to describing the way he'd made her feel was remembering the first time she'd sailed through the air after releasing a trapeze bar—scared, exhilarated, and free of all restraints.

But there were restraints. The most obvious was, she was a doctor and he was a patient. That created an invisible line between them that couldn't be crossed. She'd have to settle for the scared and exhilarated part.

She was accustomed to male patients of all ages making passes at her. Turning down various offers and blunt propositions of all kinds had always been easy in the past, but not tonight. Saying no to Phoenix Sierra had been more difficult than it should have been. Suturing a simple cut that any first-year student could have done easily had required an astonishing amount of concentration. Touching Phoenix had been like running her hand over a magnetic field, and the jolting reactions had vibrated through her veins long after she moved away from him.

What was it about him? she wondered, not for the first time. His medical fact sheet had given her his vital statistics. She knew he was thirty-four, single, had gray eyes, black hair, was six feet one inch tall, lived in an apartment in Richmond, and was co-owner of Sierra Construction.

Nothing on his medical record gave her a clue why the sight of him should affect her breathing.

His line of work helped explain his lean, muscular frame and tanned skin, but not the tiny scars on his fingers. Even hitting his fingers with a dozen hammers wouldn't have left those minuscule marks in his flesh. She'd seen a similar pattern of scars on a man's hands when she was young. One of the clowns in her parents' carnival had been an amateur woodcarver, who'd spent hours engraving designs on pieces of wood. His hands had had those permanent slashes. Phoenix Sierra could have gotten those scars from wood carving, but he didn't seem the type of man to do something like that.

Deborah lowered her feet to the floor and stood up. She started picking up the discarded cups and other trash lying around the lounge, needing to tidy up her surroundings even though she couldn't do the same with her thoughts.

She was also fighting guilt. She had the horrible feeling it was her fault his secretary had put the chicken in his car.

Two

Phoenix's arm was still a little sore Monday morning when he arrived at the office of the Sierra Construction Company, but that wasn't why he was feeling out of sorts with himself and the world at large.

As usual, Belle was already at her desk, even though he'd arrived an hour earlier than usual. She was always the first one there no matter how early Phoenix or Denver appeared in the office. Even the advent of Stan in her life hadn't affected her punctuality. Phoenix and Denver had told her they'd be more than happy to give her some slack if she ever wanted to report in late on some days, but no such luck. She was always there to guide them through their days, whether they wanted her to or not.

Seated behind her cluttered desk, Belle was bent over a list of pricing codes, her reading glasses perched on her pert nose. As usual, at least four pencils were stuck into the wad of thick carrot-colored hair arranged in a loose knot on top of her head. Her idea of proper office apparel was a mixture of *Annie Hall* and *Hee Haw*. Today's version was a denim skirt, a white poet-style shirt worn outside the skirt and cinched at the waist with a concho belt, and a patchwork vest with an assortment of colorful buttons and decorative pins scattered down the front.

When she raised her head at the sound of the door shutting behind him, her gaze fell immediately on the white bandage around his right forearm. "Rough weekend?" she asked innocently.

"Don't be coy, Belle. Your blasted chicken ran amok and tried to gnaw off my arm."

She dropped the pencil and covered her mouth with her hand. "Oh, boss. I'm sorry."

Placing his hands on her desk, he leaned toward her. "So you admit you were the one responsible for putting that chicken from hell in my car? What were you trying to do, kill me?"

She lifted her chin. "I was just trying to show you how irritating some of your practical jokes are. You weren't supposed to get hurt, only irritated enough to realize what the rest of us go through. I am sorry."

Straightening up, he clamped his hands on his hips, then smiled. "You're forgiven."

"I am?" she asked, frowning. She gave him a suspicious look. "Why?"

"My first reaction was to fire you, but instead I'm giving you a raise."

He stepped into his office, leaving Belle staring after him with her mouth open. He shut the door; then he walked around his desk and sat down. His antique leather chair protested only slightly as he leaned back with his hands behind his head and stared at the ceiling. Extra insulation in the walls provided soundproofing, shutting out the clatter of Belle's adding machine, typewriter, and voice. Even if a bulldozer thundered by outside, no sound would filter into his office. Denver hadn't questioned Phoenix's orders for the additional insulation when they'd constructed the building. Denver was one of the few people who knew the private man behind the carefree persona Phoenix presented to the world.

He sighed heavily and let the quiet of the room settle around him. He should have gone to the cabin, he mused, instead of staying in town trying to contact a woman who didn't want to see him again. Maybe if he'd spent the day in the woods, he would have been able to figure out why he felt compelled to chase after a prize he didn't stand a chance of winning.

He was uncomfortable with this obsession to see Deborah again. She was pot roast, and he was beef jerky. She was a romantic, and he was a cynic. She liked subtle humor, and his was slapstick. The only thing they appeared to have in common was an acknowledgment of their differences.

And a strong physical attraction. He knew he wasn't mistaken about her sensual response to him or the way she resisted it. He knew women found him attractive. He would have to be naive and blind not to be aware of that, and he was neither. Deborah had implied she'd examined his fingers out of professional curiosity. But he'd seen the awareness simmering in her amber eyes.

He picked up the phone and punched out a number he knew by heart. A few minutes later he replaced the receiver and glared at it, as though it were the phone's fault he couldn't get in touch with Dr. Deborah Justin.

When he'd called the emergency room the previous day, he'd been told she wasn't on duty. He'd been told the same thing just now. He didn't begrudge Deborah her time off, but it was driving him nuts that he couldn't see her or even talk to her. It was as if she'd been a dream he'd had and wanted to have again. For a man who prided himself on facing the realities of life, it wasn't easy to accept that he could be susceptible to a fantasy.

He had to see her again, to prove to himself his reaction to her had been his imagination. She wasn't listed, though, in the Richmond phone book or in directories for any of the neighboring towns. There was a chance she was married and used her maiden name for professional reasons, but she hadn't been wearing a wedding ring. It was one of the first things he'd noticed.

There was a knock on his office door. He ignored it, even though he knew it wouldn't do any good. It would be easier to deflect a stampede of buffalo than to expect Belle to take a hint.

She tapped a second time, then a few seconds later opened the door and poked her head inside. "Boss?"

Frustration, impatience, and irritation were all contained in the one word he barked at her. "What?"

Startled by his rough tone of voice, she faltered, then pushed the door farther open and stepped into the room. "This might not be a real good time to ask, but since you've just given me a raise, I figure you have to be in a halfway decent mood."

He sighed. "What is it, Belle?"

"I need a few things fixed at my new place."

"What sort of things?"

"There's a leak under the kitchen sink and a couple of the windows stick and one of the doors doesn't close right."

"No problem." He had answered automatically; then it occurred to him to ask, "What new place?"

She shook her head in exasperation. "I moved into

a town house a week ago. Don't you remember? You arranged for a couple of the guys to help me move and told me I could use one of the company trucks."

"Right," he said absently, his gaze drifting back to the phone.

She walked up to his desk. "Boss? You okay? You keep looking at the phone as though you hate it, and you aren't really listening to me. Obviously, this isn't a good time, but you're going to be leaving for one of the job sites soon, and I figured this might be the only opportunity I have today to arrange for one of the guys to come to my house."

Giving himself a mental shake, Phoenix looked at her. "I heard everything you said. I also remember that we've told you we would build you a house so you wouldn't have to keep renting one place after another."

"I know. And I told you before and I'm telling you now, I don't want to be tied down to the responsibility of a house."

"Making arrangements to have repairs done on the house you're living in sounds like responsibility to me."

"It isn't the same thing."

He shrugged. "If you say so. Tell me when's the best time for one of the workmen to come out to your house, and I'll assign someone."

"It will have to be after I get off work. My landlady works, too, so she isn't always there during the day. She offered to hire someone to do the repairs, but I told her I'd rather have one of our people do them. That way I'll know it's been done correctly." She handed him a slip of paper. "Here's my new address. My phone number is there too."

He stood up. "I'll take care of it," he said shoving

the paper in the back pocket of his jeans. "Anything else?"

"That kid sent over from Friends of the Court yesterday might need more control than the others. I assigned him to Ralph as you instructed, but the kid's got an attitude as rough as top-grade sandpaper."

"I'll check on him today. None of the kids wear halos, or we wouldn't be getting them."

"No, they just wear chips on their shoulders."

Phoenix could argue that some of the boys had good reasons for their attitudes, but Belle knew that. She had supported the work-release program the company sponsored from the very beginning, even though she grumbled occasionally about the kids.

"I'm taking Denver's schedule as well as mine today," he said. "He and Courtney aren't getting back from Nag's Head until tonight."

"It's going to be a long day for you. The schedule is pretty full."

"Good," he muttered. Then maybe he wouldn't be thinking about a certain doctor every minute of the day, as he did yesterday. He hadn't been able to forget what Deborah had said about the chicken being her fault. Or her stunning eyes. Or how good she'd felt between his thighs.

He picked up the job-site schedule off his desk and took a hard hat from the hook near the door. "I probably won't be back until late, so I'll see you tomorrow, Belle. You know how to reach me if you need me."

"Try to remember to turn on the phone in the truck this time," she scolded. "I couldn't get a hold of you at all on Friday."

"I know," he said, grinning. "It was pure heaven to drive around without you yelling in my ear every few minutes."

He was almost out the door, when she called after him, "You won't forget about sending one of the guys out to my house, will you?"

He raised his hand in acknowledgment and kept walking. "I won't forget."

But he did.

It wasn't until Phoenix was returning to the office a little after seven that night that he remembered he was supposed to have arranged for someone to go to Belle's new home. He hit the steering wheel with the heel of his hand, but it didn't accomplish a thing. If someone didn't show up at her place to fix her leaky pipe, she would think he was holding a grudge about the chicken incident and had ignored her request on purpose.

He searched the pockets of his shirt and jeans for the slip of paper with Belle's address, finally finding it in the left back pocket of his jeans. Grabbing the car phone, he punched in her number. A busy signal bleeped irritatingly in his ear. He wasn't at all surprised her line was busy, though. If Belle was awake, she'd be talking. At least he knew she was home.

It was too late to ask his employees to do the work. He could probably find some of them at Paco's, where they'd stopped for a beer after work, but it was his fault he hadn't made the arrangements earlier. He was going to have to do the repairs himself to keep the peace in the office for a little while.

It wasn't as though he had anything else to do anyway, he thought morosely. All day he'd been restless and edgy. If he didn't know better, he would think he was depressed, and that was ridiculous. From an early age he'd tried to take life as it came without worrying too much if it didn't live up to his expectations.

It took him about twenty minutes to locate Belle's

neighborhood. The housing development was relatively new and wasn't on his street map. Luckily, Sierra Construction was building a house nearby, and he remembered having seen the street sign.

Of the six town houses built together on one side of the street, Belle's was the second from one end. He spent a few minutes finding a parking spot. All the spaces were occupied except for one at the end of the block, and it took a little maneuvering to park his big truck in it. After getting the toolbox out of the back of his truck, he walked toward Belle's town house.

Even from out on the front porch, he could hear rock music being played loudly. When ringing the bell didn't accomplish anything, he pounded instead.

The door was finally pulled open, and Belle stood gaping at him as though he were Santa Claus—or maybe it was Jack the Ripper.

"Boss! What are you doing here?"

He held up his toolbox. "Your friendly neighborhood handyman at your service."

"You forgot to ask someone to do the repairs, didn't you?" she said, stepping back to allow him into her home.

"You know me so well. Where's the kitchen?" he asked as his long strides carried him through the living room, following a path between assorted cardboard boxes. "Never mind. I found it. Nice place, Belle."

"It will be once I get everything put away." Following him, she watched as he opened the doors under the sink. "You didn't have to come tonight, boss. It isn't really that urgent."

He hefted the full pail of water from under the sink. "I wouldn't say that."

It didn't take him long to fix the leak under the

sink. A couple of turns on one of the connections with a crescent wrench took care of it. He moved on to the windows, refusing Belle's offer of a drink. All he wanted to do was get the repairs done and go home, although the thought of going back to his empty apartment wasn't very appealing. Spending a quiet night alone hadn't bothered him before. In fact, he usually preferred it, but tonight, the very idea irritated the hell out of him.

The first stuck window was no problem. A little planing on the wood frame and a minor adjustment on the sliding mechanism did the trick. The second one, the living-room window facing the street, wasn't so easy. He wrestled with it, finally getting it open, then settled in to fix the problem.

As he shifted position, he nudged a couple of the tools he'd set on the windowsill. They started to slide off toward the outside. There was no screen on the window, so he made a grab for them. As he reached, some movement out on the street caught his eye, and he looked up.

A woman was walking up the sidewalk of the town house next door. A woman with copper-colored hair, long legs, and swaying slender hips that made his mouth go dry. The shock of recognition had him straightening up, and his head struck the bottom of the open window.

The next thing he knew, he was sitting on the floor leaning against the wall. Aside from his bemusement at finding himself in such a position, he realized he had one king-sized headache. There was also something cold and heavy on his head. Reaching up, he felt an ice bag. It wasn't helping the pain, since it hadn't been placed over the lump caused by his hard head coming in contact with the even harder window frame.

Cursing under his breath, he planted his hand on the floor and put some weight on his arm, preparing to stand up. He swore again when the stitches in his forearm protested the strain. Still, he was starting to push himself up, when his secretary's angry voice had him hesitating.

"Dammit, boss. Stay put," Belle ordered as she rushed into the living room. "You might have a concussion. Luckily, my landlady just came home and is willing to take a look at your head."

"Tell her to go away. I'm fine," he muttered as he continued to struggle to his feet.

A voice he was beginning to think he would never hear again answered him. "I see a run-in with a window didn't knock any sense into you."

"Deborah," he murmured, wondering if he was still unconscious and dreaming. He blinked, then simply stared.

Belle looked from her boss to her landlady. "You two know each other?"

"In a manner of speaking," Deborah replied. "We met in the emergency room Saturday night."

Phoenix kept staring at her, still not sure he wasn't seeing only what he wanted to see. But she was very real. Her legs, encased in snug denim jeans, seemed to go on forever as she walked toward him. In her right hand, she carried a leather satchel. His gaze slid upward, to a white chiffon shirt with small navy polka dots scattered on the sleeves and collar. The material was transparent enough for him to see lace covering her breasts.

At the hospital he'd wondered how her hair would look loose. His imagination hadn't lived up to the real thing. Her reddish-brown hair surrounded her face in a silky riot that made him ache to run his fingers through the thick, luxurious strands. It made him ache for other things as well. The thought of how her hair would feel on his bare skin did invigorating things to his system.

Considering the direction his thoughts were going, his first words to her were unusually harsh. "Where in the hell have you been?"

It was her turn to blink and stare. She stopped a few feet away from him. "Excuse me?"

"You haven't been at work for the last two days."

"I'm aware of that," she answered evenly. "Even doctors get days off."

"You aren't in the phone book either."

She closed the distance between them and knelt down beside him. Placing her fingers on his wrist, she took his pulse. "You keep telling me things I already know."

His heart had started racing the moment he'd looked up and seen her. When she touched him, he could feel his blood accelerate through his veins and throb in his loins.

As she bent her head to look at her watch, something Belle had said filtered through his bemused brain. "You're Belle's landlady?"

"Hmm," she murmured. A few seconds later she raised her head, surprise widening her eyes. "Your pulse is very rapid."

"I'm not a bit surprised," he drawled. "You have that effect on me."

She opened her case, ignoring his provocative statement. Taking out a small flashlight, she directed the narrow beam into each of his eyes. Evidently satisfied with what she found, she leaned forward to examine his most recent injury.

"Would you lean forward a little?" she asked.

By doing that, Phoenix wouldn't be able to look into her eyes, something he very much wanted to do for at least the next year or so. However, when he moved forward, he realized his mouth was only inches away from her breasts. Her scent slashed through him. Jasmine and woman—a heady combination. When she ran her fingers through his hair, gently searching for any injury, he thought he was going to lose all control. It wouldn't take much more for him to grab her and pull her down to the floor under him.

She found the lump and examined it carefully. "You haven't broken the skin. Are you nauseated?"

He shook his head, but that hurt, so he stopped. "No, but I have a pip of a headache."

"I'm not surprised. You've quite a good-sized knot on your head. It might be a good idea if you go to the emergency room and have an X ray ta—"

"No! No more emergency rooms. It's just a knock on the head. No big deal. I have a hard head."

Her eyes glittered with amusement, and she didn't disagree with his last comment. "I'll give you something for the headache."

"I don't need anything." When she started to move away, he grasped her wrist. "Where are you going?"

Sitting back on her heels, she easily twisted her arm out of his grip. "I'm going home. You aren't taking any of my advice, so I'm wasting my time."

He threw an arm up to his forehead and sank back against the wall in a dramatic imitation of a swoon. "I don't feel very well. You can't leave yet."

Deborah looked up at Belle, who was rolling her eyes toward the ceiling. When she brought her gaze back to her patient, she saw that his eyes were shut, his arm still over his forehead.

"Well," she said as she began rummaging around

in her satchel. "Maybe this is more serious than I thought. What's needed here is a shot to make you feel better. Where's the big needle? I was sure I packed one in here just for this kind of emergency."

His eyes snapped open. "How big a needle?"

"A really big needle. It'll make the pain go away."

"I don't need a shot," he said as he sat up. "It doesn't hurt that much."

She smiled. "See how well it works." She patted his shoulder. "You have a very hard head in more ways than one, Mr. Sierra. You're going to live."

He glared at her. "You're giving me one giant pain by continuing to call me Mr. Sierra."

She pursed her lips. "I guess I owe you that much. All right—Phoenix. Are you satisfied?"

He grinned. "Gratified maybe. Not satisfied. That will come later."

Getting to her feet, she turned to Belle. "Does he usually ramble like this without making a lot of sense?"

Belle shrugged. "Pretty much, yeah."

"I didn't connect him with the stories you've been telling me about your employers. You always referred to them as 'boss,' no matter which one you were talking about."

Before Belle could comment, Phoenix said, "Would you two stop talking about me as though I'm not here?"

The two women looked down at him with similarly tolerant expressions on their faces. Feeling as though he was being treated like a misbehaving child, he started to get to his feet. A sudden dizziness had him grasping for the windowsill.

"Boss!" Belle exclaimed. She grabbed one arm, and Deborah took the other. Together they helped him over to the couch. It was obvious that this time he wasn't faking it.

He made a sound of relief as he sank down on the cushions. Fighting the waves of light-headedness, he leaned back and closed his eyes.

Deborah bit her lip, feeling guilty for underestimating his injury. "Belle, would you get a washcloth and rinse it out in cold water, please?"

Leaning over Phoenix, she lifted one of his eyelids to examine his reaction to light, then checked the other. His dark gaze locked with hers, obvious arousal blending with exhaustion and pain. When Belle hurried back, Deborah looked away from him to take the cloth. She folded it several times before placing it on the back of Phoenix's neck.

Belle hovered over them. "Is there anything else I can do?"

"Would you bring a glass of water, please?" Deborah said.

"You got it."

The cushion gave a little when Deborah sat down beside Phoenix. Turned sideways to face him, she lifted his wrist between her forefinger and thumb to take his pulse again.

"My heart's fine," he said huskily, closing his eyes once more. Maybe, he thought, if he couldn't see her, he wouldn't want her so much. It didn't work, though, not when she spoke. Her voice was low with a husky, intimate tone that had his body hardening and his heart softening.

"Your pulse is a little erratic," she said.

He opened his eyes and met her concerned gaze. "It's not going to get any better as long as you're touching me."

She released his wrist. "I'm sorry I didn't take your

injury seriously. That was wrong. For a doctor, it's unforgivable."

This time he took her wrist, his thumb stroking across the delicate bones. He was pleased to feel her pulse accelerate. He wasn't the only one affected by the swiftly building attraction between them.

"From now on," he said, "maybe you'll take me seriously."

She sighed. "I hope this is the last time you need a doctor. At least for a few days."

"That's not what I meant. I want you to take *me* seriously, not my injuries."

Her mouth curved into a mocking smile. "I'm supposed to take a man who puts goldfish in water coolers seriously?"

"That's what I do, not who I am."

Deborah frowned as her gaze scanned his face. She had the feeling there was more truth in what he'd just said than he might have wanted her to hear.

"Mr. Sierra," she began, then hesitated, not sure what else she wanted to say.

He took a deep breath. "You're inflicting another injury against me now, Dr. Justin. You already said you'd call me Phoenix."

"I really am sorry if I seemed to be making fun of you."

Spreading her fingers out against his hand, he said softly, "Don't be so hard on yourself. I just had a moment of dizziness, that's all. It could be more from hunger and lack of sleep than a lump on the head. I haven't eaten all day, and I haven't gotten much sleep the last couple of nights."

"That's not very smart."

A corner of his mouth lifted slightly. "Probably not.

Are you going to tell me you manage to have regular meals when you're on duty at the hospital?"

"No, but—"

"It's the same thing. I was too busy today to take time out to eat. Not that it would have mattered if I did have the time. I seem to have lost my appetite and the ability to sleep since I looked up and saw you in the emergency room. All I've managed to accomplish these past two days was to think about you and to feel like hitting something when I couldn't find you." He lifted his hand to his head. "This is your fault too. I was so surprised to see you walking toward the town house next door, I banged my head on the window and knocked myself out."

Deborah looked away from him, unnerved by the steady intensity of his eyes. Glancing down, she saw his scarred fingers were laced in and around hers, creating an involuntary warmth low in her body.

"Perhaps . . ." She paused to clear her throat. "Perhaps it would be safer for you not to have me around."

"I'll take the chance," he murmured. "But it might be a good idea for you to bring your medical bag along when we go out, just in case."

"I'm not going out with you," she said as sternly as she could. It was really unfortunate that her voice still shook slightly.

He smiled. "We don't have to go out. I'd be perfectly happy to stay in with you, although I should warn you. It will be harder for me to keep my hands off you if we're alone."

His smile captivated her. She clenched her hand to keep herself from touching his mouth, realizing too late that she was tightening her fingers around his.

Her desire to touch him in other than a professional manner startled her. So did her reaction to his obvious interest in her.

One of the conclusions she'd made when he'd come on to her in the emergency room was that he took very little in life seriously. She was the complete opposite. She took her work and herself extremely seriously. That was the result of growing up in a family that made its living from fun and games.

That difference alone made any idea of getting involved with Phoenix Sierra ludicrous.

Even if she had the time and the inclination, he wasn't her type of man. Yet despite her reasoning, she had trouble resisting the appeal in his charming smile and piercing eyes.

Belle returned with the glass of water, saving Deborah from having to respond to Phoenix's provocative statement. She gestured for Belle to give the water to Phoenix. After she asked him the routine questions about allergies, she tugged her hand away from his and took a bottle of pain medication out of her satchel. She dropped two pills into his hand, then snapped her satchel shut.

"I'm probably wasting my breath," she said, "but you really should eat something."

He swallowed the pills. "Where would you like to go?"

She shook her head, admiration for his persistence making her smile. "I was talking about you, not me."

"I'm talking about us."

She raised a brow and glanced at Belle. "You never told me your employer had a hearing problem."

"He hears what he wants to hear," Belle said. "The word 'no' isn't part of his vocabulary as a general rule."

"I'm beginning to understand that."

Phoenix looked from one to the other, then frowned at Belle. "You're about to lose that raise I gave you this morning. What have you been telling her about me?"

She held up her hand in a placating gesture. "Nothing but the truth."

He smiled wryly. "No wonder she doesn't want to go out with me. I suppose you've filled her head with horror stories of how Denver and I work your little fingers to the bone."

"And how you've had me send flowers to scores of women after your involvement with them is over."

"That's a big help," he grumbled.

He took the washcloth and tossed it onto a nearby cardboard box. Placing his hand on the arm of the couch, he pushed himself up, grimacing as his injured arm protested. Once he was standing, he looked down at Deborah. "I haven't known you very long, but you impress me as a woman who can make up her own mind instead of letting others do it for her."

"I have made up my mind. You and I don't have anything in common, so it would be a waste of time to pretend we do by seeing each other."

Her words sounded pretty final, but Phoenix wasn't about to accept them. "How do you know we have nothing in common unless we spend some time together?"

Deborah opened her mouth to answer, but at that moment she saw him frown and rub the back of his neck. His face was still alarmingly pale, despite his tan. Standing, she took his arm. It didn't require a medical degree to know that he wasn't feeling all that great. She knew he wouldn't take her advice, either, for he hadn't listened to much of what she'd said so far. She would just have to find a way around his stubbornness.

"Belle," she said, turning to the other woman, "you and I are going to take Phoenix home. Do you know where he lives?"

Three

Each woman took an arm and stayed at his side as they guided him to the front door. He might as well have saved his breath when he said he didn't need their help, Phoenix thought. They were like two runaway trains with full heads of steam, and he was the caboose being pulled along for the ride.

Belle closed and locked the door behind them, then they walked down to the street. Without discussing it, they bypassed Belle's tiny Volkswagen. Phoenix went along without protesting, until they stopped beside the small compact car parked in Deborah's driveway.

"You don't really expect me to get into that tin can, do you?" he asked, as Deborah took out her keys.

"Well, you could run alongside," she said. "But I think under the circumstances you might have a little difficulty keeping up."

Sliding his hand into a front pocket of his jeans, he withdrew a ring of keys. "You can ride with me in my truck," he said, feeling very pleased with himself that he'd come up with the perfect solution to get her to go with him.

She grabbed the keys out of his hand. "Right. You can ride with me in your truck."

He clamped his hands on his hips and confronted her. "No one drives my truck but me."

"There's a first time for everything." She took his arm again and nodded to Belle to do the same. "You need to get home and rest, so either I drive your truck or you squash into my tin can."

"Deborah," he began, then forgot what he was arguing about when she slung his arm over her shoulder and tucked herself into his side. Her soft breast pressed against his ribs. Several strands of her hair brushed his neck, making his mind run along a completely different track than how he was going to get home.

As they neared his truck, he forced himself back on track. "I'm serious, Deborah. I don't want you driving my truck."

"That's unfortunate, but also irrelevant if you want to get home. Although there is one other option."

"What?" he asked, ready to grab any alternative.

"I could call an ambulance and have you taken to the hospital for observation."

He raised his chin and scowled down his chiseled nose at her. "You have a mean streak in you, Doc. Any other time I might appreciate that."

She patted his midsection in a patronizing fashion. "Look at it this way. You probably have the only doctor in Virginia willing to make a house call. Consider yourself fortunate and quit complaining."

She slipped out from under his arm and unlocked the passenger side of his Bronco. Opening the door, she gestured for him to get in. When he didn't, she planted herself in front of him and crossed her arms over her chest.

"Look," she said, "I've driven eighteen-wheelers and operated a forklift and a pile driver. I've even pulled an elephant in a cage behind a truck that was a helluva lot more powerful than yours. I don't think your itty-bitty old Bronco will give me any problems."

It was a toss-up who was more stunned by her outburst, Phoenix or Belle. They both stared at her for nearly a full minute. She waited, her gaze never leaving Phoenix. A gust of wind tousled her hair around her face, but she didn't seem to notice.

Phoenix did. He was reminded of the only painting hanging in his apartment. Though the woman in the painting was an American Indian with black hair, and was wearing only a brief piece of deerskin as she stood on the crest of a cliff, Deborah looked like that proud woman. The stance was the same, the confident tilt of the head, the majestic beauty, the suggestion of untamed sensuality.

"Oh, hell!" he mumbled. It was a testament to how lousy he felt and how Deborah affected him that he actually gave in. "Drive the damn truck."

Belle let go of his arm and covered her mouth with her hand to keep from laughing out loud. A good secretary never laughed at her employer, at least not in his presence.

As Deborah walked around the front of the Bronco, Belle called to her, "You follow me, and I'll show you where he lives. Then, after we tuck him in nice and cozy, you can ride back with me."

Phoenix started to turn his head to glare at Belle. The action didn't do his headache much good, so he gave it up. Once he'd levered himself into the passenger seat and slammed the door, he turned his attention to the woman sliding behind the wheel. Of his truck.

She met his wary gaze and took pity on him.

Reaching across him, she pulled the seat belt around him and clicked it into place. Then she patted his leg and said gently, "Relax. This won't hurt a bit. I'm really a very good driver."

He looked down to where her hand had touched his thigh. It didn't hurt at all. Damned if it didn't feel as if he'd been branded, though. And she wasn't even touching him any longer. He wished she would. Touch him everywhere all night long and into the morning.

She was moving away from him when he flung his hand out to stop her. Cupping the back of her neck, he brought her back to him. "I'm hurting, Doc," he said in a low, husky voice. "Make me feel better."

Deborah opened her mouth to protest, but whatever she was going to say was halted by Phoenix kissing her. Her first instinct was to pull away. But though his grip wasn't hurting her, it was firm enough to hold her in place. And that place was alarmingly close to him. He wasn't testing, or teasing, or tentative as he slanted his mouth over hers. He was aroused and hungry and not shy about communicating that.

When she felt herself responding to the naked longing in his kiss, Deborah raised her hand to push against his chest. Instead her fingers clenched around his shirt as his tongue sought the intimacy of her mouth. The yearning sound she heard startled her. It had come from her.

She jerked away from him, careful even in her panic not to hurt him. To her relief he released her. Moving over on the seat, she gripped the steering wheel tightly.

"Do you feel better?" she asked, and cringed inwardly at the hoarseness in her voice.

"Not a lot, no."

Deborah was thankful to see Belle backing out her driveway at that moment. Shoving in the ignition key, she started the engine, then pulled out into the street. It required an astonishing amount of control for her not to press the accelerator to the floor. It wouldn't have done any good anyway. She couldn't outrun the cause of her tension. He was in the truck with her.

When the fenders of his Bronco remained intact after the first mile, Phoenix began to relax. A little. Deborah hadn't exaggerated, he admitted begrudgingly. She was a more than competent driver. It still rankled that she was the one driving his truck, but not as much as he'd thought it would. It had always been important for him to be in control, whether it was behind the wheel of a vehicle, in his business dealings, or in his personal relationships. Since meeting Deborah, he hadn't been able to dominate the situation at all.

His gaze drifted down to her hand, as she changed gears with an easy motion. "How is it that a medical doctor knows how to drive an eighteen-wheeler?" he asked.

She didn't look at him, but kept her attention on the road and Belle's car. "It's one of those things I picked up when I was young."

"You make it sound like you're ancient. How far back did this wild turn behind the wheel take place?"

"In another world," she said vaguely.

"You have the control of my truck and all my attention. Tell me about this other world."

Stopping at a red light, she flicked a glance in his direction. "You already have a headache. Why add boredom to it?"

"Deborah, nothing about you could be remotely boring. Frustrating, perhaps. Beautiful, definitely.

Maybe a bit mystifying—but not boring. I can honestly say I don't know any other woman who is proficient at driving an eighteen-wheeler, much less one who even knows what a pile driver is."

"There aren't a lot of us around."

He appreciated her dry humor but not what her words implied. "You're not going to tell me, are you?"

"It doesn't look like it."

He started to grimace ruefully, then stopped when the movement of his lips reminded him of the kiss he'd stolen a few minutes ago. "We'll save the story of your life for another time, then. I can wait."

"You're going to have a long wait, because there won't be another time."

He didn't like the note of finality in her voice, and he wasn't about to accept it. "Do you have something against dating in general, or is it dating me that you're objecting to? And don't tell me you're too busy. You weren't at the hospital yesterday or today, so you do have some free time."

"Sorry to disappoint you, but I was working today and yesterday too."

"Not at the hospital. I called." He had another thought, one he didn't particularly like. "Unless you told whoever answers the phone to tell me you weren't there."

She made an unladylike sound. "No wonder you hit your head. It's swelled up to twice the size it should be. Why in the world would you think where I am or what I do is any of your business?"

He sighed and closed his eyes, laying his head back on the seat. "Beats me. It just is."

Deborah frowned, surprised by the resigned, almost defeated tone in his voice. She'd expected a joking rejoinder, a teasing remark, a flip reply. Instead she'd been given an answer that completely shook her.

She chanced a glance in his direction while waiting for another stoplight to change. His eyes were closed, and she saw faint frown lines between them. As a doctor, she would have said they were caused by the headache. As a woman, she wondered if it wasn't something completely different. He had, simply and succinctly, admitted how he felt about her, without pressuring her either to believe him or to admit the same.

If he'd given her an honest answer this time, it was possible he'd been truthful with her from the beginning. If that was so, then he was genuinely interested in her, and not just giving her a line. She wasn't sure how she felt about that. It had been easier to turn him down when she thought he was simply coming on to her as an automatic response. If he was serious, that made the situation thoroughly different and confusing—and tempting.

Since he'd been honest with her, she should at least be honest with herself. She was attracted to him. Something about him drew her, excited her, made her feel feminine, desirable. Even though he wasn't aware of it, he had made her do unexpected things. Like telling him about driving eighteen-wheelers, and becoming personally involved with a patient to the point of driving him home. She rarely talked about her life growing up in a carnival, even indirectly. It wasn't because she was ashamed of the way she'd grown up, but because people generally didn't understand what she was talking about.

Nor had she ever kissed a patient. Technically, Phoenix wasn't her patient, but she'd definitely kissed him.

The sound of a horn blaring behind them brought

her attention back to the traffic light, which had turned green. As she stepped on the gas and shifted, she was aware that Phoenix had opened his eyes and was looking at her. It took a great deal of concentration for her to keep from meeting his gaze, but even so, she felt as if he were touching her. She didn't like the intensity of the current that flowed between them, nor did she understand it. But she knew it was there.

Ahead, Belle had turned on her left turn signal, indicating she was going to enter the parking area sprawled around a tall apartment building. Following the little car, Deborah found a place to park. She reached behind the seat for her medical bag, then opened her door and dropped down from the high seat to the pavement. By the time she had walked around the truck, Phoenix had also gotten out and was leaning against the front fender, his arms crossed over his chest, his gaze fixed on the entrance of the building.

The way he was concentrating on the building made Deborah think he might be wondering if he could make it that far. The bump on his head wasn't serious, but combined with a lack of sleep and not eating all day, it was understandable if he felt a little weak.

She stopped near him and noticed that he was squinting, as though the sun were in his eyes. In fact, the sun had gone down already. A slight breeze ruffled his dark hair, and she saw him shiver even though it was a mild night. She resisted taking his arm, sensing that he would resent her offer of support. Instead she held his keys out to him.

Phoenix heard the soft clatter of keys and turned to look at Deborah. He pushed away from the fender and closed one hand around her hand and his keys.

With the other hand he took the keys. His gaze was unrelenting as he looked down at her.

"You're not leaving," he said softly, making it a demand and not a question.

"No," she said, and added, "I'm not leaving yet."

He started walking toward the apartment building, keeping the possessive grip on her hand. Belle was already waiting for them near the entrance. Deborah caught Belle glancing at their clasped hands, but for once the outspoken woman managed to keep her thoughts to herself.

Phoenix didn't release her hand as they all rode the elevator up four floors. Usually, Belle would have filled the silence with chatter, but she obviously was as aware as Deborah of Phoenix's need for some peace and quiet.

He leaned against the back wall of the elevator, his eyes closed to block out the fluorescent lighting overhead. He opened them again when the elevator reached his floor. Bringing Deborah along with him, he walked down the hall to apartment 416 and unlocked the door.

Still he didn't let go of Deborah's hand. His grip was possessive, and not, she knew, because he wanted her assistance. Deborah sensed it would require more than a bump on the head to make Phoenix Sierra helpless. He was hurting, hungry, and tired, but by no stretch of the imagination would she think he was helpless.

Pushing the door open, he stepped aside to let Belle enter first, then drew Deborah in front of him so she would precede him. As he walked into the small foyer, he reached beyond Deborah's shoulder and flicked on a light switch.

Belle planted her hands on her hips and looked

around the living room. She whistled under her breath, then turned, grinning, to Deborah.

"Ain't it somethin'? This is the type of place my mama warned me about."

Phoenix started to tell Belle what she could do with her opinions, but changed his mind as soon as he said her name. The simple act of speaking sent slivers of pain stabbing his head. It just wasn't worth it. After all, Belle wasn't the first person to exclaim loudly over his decor.

He wondered, though, what Deborah's reaction would be. Generally, he didn't care a fig about other people's opinions, but he was suddenly very concerned about hers. Part of him, the sane part, wanted her to hate it. The other part, the lonely part, wanted her to understand.

Primed by Belle's comment, Deborah looked around the living room with interest. The furniture and carpet were red. Not a deep cherry red or a poppy red. The color was more a fire-engine red—complete with siren. If it wasn't for the black throw pillows and glass and chrome tables, that intense red would be all anyone saw. A large curved sofa took up most of the room, its cushions plush and opulent. Against one wall stood a large entertainment center with every conceivable electrical gadget, from a large-screen television set with a VCR on top to a CD player.

As Deborah took in the extensive array of CDs, videotapes, and record albums, she wondered if all the equipment was for the entertainment of other people, or for a man who spent a great deal of time alone. Even though she couldn't explain why she thought so, she decided everything was for Phoenix's use, not to impress anyone else.

What held her attention the longest was a painting

on one wall that depicted an Indian maiden standing on the edge of a cliff looking out at the desert below. The woman's long black hair was blowing wildly in the wind as she stood proudly on the cliff, wearing only a tight piece of deerskin that covered her breasts and belly and skimmed the tops of her thighs. Deborah felt her throat tighten with emotion. The painting was the most powerful original work of art she'd ever seen.

"Well?"

Puzzled by Phoenix's flat question, she turned her head to look at him. "Well, what?"

His gaze narrowed as he studied her carefully. "You haven't pulled any punches yet. Why start now?"

"I wouldn't think of hitting a man when he's down and almost out, especially when I didn't understand why he's expecting it." She glanced at Belle, then back at Phoenix. Neither one had moved. "Is there some sort of password we have to say before we go farther into your apartment, or is this as far as you allow people to go?"

A faint sigh of relief escaped Phoenix. She really didn't know what he was talking about. Maybe it was time for him to stop putting her in the same category as other people.

Feeling she deserved an explanation, he said, "I usually have to put up with various comments on my lack of taste when someone sees my apartment for the first time. I was waiting for yours."

Something, some powerful emotion, she barely glimpsed in the depths of his eyes, held Deborah spellbound for a few seconds. Then it was gone. It really mattered to him what she thought of his apartment, she realized. Why, she didn't know. But if he really wanted to hear her opinion, she would oblige. Otherwise, they might all be standing there for the next hour.

"I once knew a Gypsy fortune-teller," she said, "who lived in a trailer that had purple velvet wallpaper, a tiger-skin rug on the floor, tassels hanging down from the windows, and drop crystal lampshades. She also had a Ph.D. in economics and had written two books before giving up her life as a professor to travel with a circus. Compared to her place, this is a walk in the park. Everything I've seen so far is for effect." Shifting her gaze to the painting, she added, "Except for that painting. That's the only part of the furnishings that's for you."

Phoenix's breath left his body as though he'd been hit in the stomach with a two-by-four. His hand tightened around hers, but she misunderstood the reason for that.

"Belle," she said, "why don't you see what the kitchen has to offer in the way of food. Something light. Eggs, toast, or soup."

Like a runner who'd been waiting for the starting pistol, Belle took off in the direction of the kitchen. Deborah brought her attention back to Phoenix as he leaned against the wall. Untangling her fingers from his, she ignored his dark protesting glance and slid her arm around his waist.

"Let's go find your bed. You look like you've been washed twice and hung out to dry."

He made a choking sound that ended up as amusement. "Why, Doc. How you talk." His arm came around her shoulders. "As much as I like your invitation, I think I should remind you we aren't alone." He sighed soulfully. "I should have fired Belle when I had the chance."

"I said you need a bed, not *we* need a bed."

"Darn," he muttered.

Deborah felt his weight sag against her as they walked through the living room toward the hall that obviously led to his bedroom. Two of the three doors along the hall were open. The first one revealed an opulently furnished bathroom, and the one across the hall led to his bedroom. Having found what she'd been looking for, she didn't bother asking about the third room.

Entering his bedroom, she was relieved to see the furnishings were more in keeping with a bedroom than a bordello. The light trailing from the hallway revealed brick-red walls, dark furniture, and a king-sized bed covered with a rust-and-black paisley comforter. Covering part of the wood floor was an Oriental carpet in dark colors.

She stopped at the side of the bed and stepped back, ignoring his look of irritation at the distance she was putting between them. Placing her hands on his shoulders, she gently pressed until he obeyed her unspoken command and sat down on the bed.

Before she could move away, he shackled her wrist with his hand. "I don't want you to leave."

She gave in to the desire to touch him by brushing his windblown hair back from his forehead. Without realizing she was going to say it, she gave him what he wanted. "I'll be here when you wake up."

"Good," he murmured. He released her wrist and lay down on his side. "If you left, I'd have to come after you, and I don't feel much like it at the moment."

"Those late-night parties will get you every time," she said. She kept her voice light, though she was annoyed with herself both for giving in to him and for wanting to stay in the first place.

She heard him make a disgruntled sound, but she didn't know if it was directed at her comment or the partying itself. He closed his eyes, and she walked across the room to draw the drapes. When she turned back, his breathing was already deep and relaxed. Returning to the bed, she said his name softly. His only response was to turn his head slowly on the pillow, as though trying to find a comfortable position. He didn't open his eyes.

She glanced at her watch, figuring out how long it had been since she'd checked his eye response. She could wait to check it again. Stepping around to the foot of the bed, she unlaced his heavy work boots and tugged them off. His only reaction was a slight frown. She debated removing any of his clothes, then decided against it. If he was uncomfortable, he was going to have to undress himself. It wasn't that she was a prude, but she was cautious.

Clothed, Phoenix Sierra was a sensual threat. Stripped, he would be an irresistible temptation.

She laid the back of her hand against his forehead, noting he wasn't overly warm. Trailing her hand lightly across his temple, she ran several fingers through his thick, glossy hair. Touching him had nothing to do with her profession and everything to do with sensuous pleasure. She could make up a dozen excuses for why she had brought him home rather than letting him fend for himself. Belle and even Phoenix might believe she was just being an efficient physician, reaching out to someone who needed her. She knew, though, that she was there because Phoenix made her feel things she didn't understand, and it was important for her to figure them out. She barely knew him other than a few vital statistics. That was only surface knowledge, nothing concrete about the man inside. Yet she was beginning to suspect he had an inner sensitivity that he covered with practical jokes and quick quips. She needed to discover more about him, even though her instincts were screaming at her that he could cause her great problems if she wasn't careful.

She heard him take a deep, shuddering breath and murmur her name. She drew back her hand. For a few minutes more she simply stood by the bed and watched him sleep. She was oddly content just to look at him. And that scared her.

A faint sound finally made her remember she wasn't alone in his apartment. With one last glance at him, she turned abruptly and left his bedroom.

When she reached the kitchen, she only got as far as the doorway, then stopped and stared. "Belle, what in the world are you doing?"

Before answering, Belle found a spot on the counter where she could fit a box of cereal. It wasn't that easy to find, since Belle herself was kneeling on the counter between the sink and the refrigerator, and all around her were canned goods, spices, and assorted containers of foodstuffs.

"You told me to find something for the boss to eat," Belle said. "While I was looking, I decided to reorganize the stuff I found in his cupboards. How's he doing?"

"He's asleep. He said he hadn't slept much the last couple of days, and I guess he wasn't just trying for sympathy. He's evidently exhausted from partying all night and working all day."

Belle didn't seem all that concerned about Phoenix as she started stuffing groceries back into the cupboards. In alphabetical order. "I'm sure he hasn't slept much lately. I know he and Stan were out most of Friday night looking for a runaway. He could have been up with one of his kids last night too."

"His kids? Phoenix has children?"

Hearing the shock in Deborah's voice, Belle shifted

on the counter until she was sitting facing Deborah, her legs dangling over the edge. "Not his kids as in his own children. I just call them that instead of hoodlums or delinquents, because those labels make him mad."

Deborah leaned her hip against the kitchen table, suddenly needing the extra support. Her legs seemed a little wobbly at the moment. "He works with kids who are in trouble?"

Belle nodded. "It started when a boy and his girlfriend broke into Courtney Sierra's house. Actually, she was Courtney Caine then." Changing mental gears, she added, "Did you know Denver's mother-in-law is Amethyst Rand, the country-western singer?"

"No, I didn't know that."

Belle nodded again, vigorously. "Courtney's two sisters sing too. You've heard of the Jewels of the South? That's her sisters and their mother. All of them have the names of jewels, you see."

When Belle stopped to take a breath, Deborah quickly said, "You were saying something about Phoenix's—ah, kids?"

"Right. The break-in happened before Courtney married Denver and was caused by true love not running smoothly for the teenagers. They blamed Courtney for giving Romeo a failing grade, which he deserved but which meant they couldn't see each other."

Feeling as though she were sinking into quicksand, Deborah attempted to hang on to the original subject. "What do these teenagers have to do with Phoenix?"

"I was getting to that," Belle said with a trace of irritation. "Instead of having the boy turned over to the authorities, Courtney asked Denver and Phoenix to find him some work to do as a way for him to earn the money to pay for the damages to her house.

When Phoenix saw how beneficial it was for the teenager to work off his debt and some of his aggression on honest labor, he got together with a youth counselor, and they started a program called Friends of the Court. Stan and some of his cop buddies occasionally call Phoenix when there's a runaway or a kid in trouble somewhere who would benefit from Phoenix's program. Sometimes he's out all night driving around looking for some kid or other. There've been a lot of nights Phoenix doesn't get any sleep, then works a full day."

Deborah looked away. She didn't want Phoenix to be a sensitive, caring man. She wanted him to be a party animal, a womanizer with the morals of an alley cat. That would make it so much easier to dismiss her attraction to him. She needed all the defenses she could muster against him, but her preconceived notions were being knocked away. Now she had to readjust her opinion about him, which put her defenses all out of kilter.

"I see," she said inadequately. "You can forget about fixing any food for Phoenix." Joining Belle at the counter, she began to stack the cans and boxes back into the cupboards. "I'm going to stay here the rest of the night and wake him every two hours to make sure he isn't suffering any ill effects from the concussion."

Belle frowned at the mess Deborah was making of her system and moved the food containers to where she wanted them. "Do you want me to stay here with you?"

Shaking her head, Deborah gave up trying to help Belle. "It's silly for both of us to lose sleep. You go on home. Since his latest trip to the emergency room was more or less my fault, I should be the one to stay."

"Your fault? Why do you say that?"

"The night you moved in next door to me, you brought a bottle of champagne over along with your first rent check. Halfway through the bottle, you told me about one of your bosses who kept pulling practical jokes on you. I vaguely remember telling you about some of the pranks med students used to torture each other with. One of them was about a car that had a dozen frogs in it."

Jumping down from the counter, Belle grinned at Deborah. "I had to substitute a chicken. Couldn't find any frogs."

"Still, I gave you the general idea, and I feel responsible—so I'm staying with Phoenix tonight."

"Do you want me to come by for you in the morning?"

She shook her head. "I don't have to be at the hospital until noon. I'll either call a cab or ask Phoenix to drive me home on his way to work in the morning."

"If I didn't need my beauty sleep or if I knew anything about medicine, I would argue with you, but you're the doctor." Belle paused in her rearranging of groceries and gave Deborah an odd look. "Are you sure you want to stay here alone with Phoenix? He might be exhausted, but he's not dead."

Deborah smiled. "You don't have a thing to worry about. I'm here for professional reasons, not personal ones. You won't be sending me flowers in a couple of weeks. I'm not getting involved with your boss."

Belle tilted her head to one side. "Maybe you already are and just don't know it."

Deborah gave her a look she usually reserved for incompetent staff and unreasonable patients. "I'm not, and I know it."

"You could do worse," Belle murmured under her breath.

Deborah heard her. Privately, she had to agree, but she would never admit it. Phoenix Sierra was turning out to be more than she'd expected, and her reaction was more than she liked.

Four

By the time Deborah finished helping Belle stuff the contents of the cupboards back and ushered her out the door, it was a little after ten o'clock. Time to wake up Phoenix and check his responses.

When she touched his shoulder, shaking him gently, he grunted. She couldn't help smiling at his grouchiness but still insisted on his waking. "Tell me your name, Phoenix."

He opened one eye—sort of. "Why? You already know it. You just said it."

"I want to hear you say it."

A martyred sigh came before he muttered, "Phoenix Sky Sierra."

She bit back a laugh with difficulty. "Sky?"

He opened both eyes. "It's not nice to make fun of a man's name, Doc," he said with mock severity.

"I was merely commenting on your unusual middle name. Silly of me, I suppose, considering your other names."

"Fair is fair. What's your middle name?"

"I don't have one."

His eyes widened, his expression indicating his astonishment. "Everybody has a middle name."

"Not me."

"Why not?"

She shrugged. "My mother wanted to give me an unpronounceable Bulgarian, name and my father wanted me to have his mother's name, which was Armintina. Lucky for me, they hadn't come to any agreement by the time the hospital demanded my birth certificate be filled out."

"How about a nickname? Give me something here, Deborah."

"I'm just too dull for words. And I'm supposed to be the one asking the questions." She directed the light into his eyes. "Don't shut your eyes."

"Sorry. It's what I do when a bright light is suddenly shined in them."

He remained still long enough for her to see his pupils contract correctly. Satisfied, she turned off the small flashlight. "Now you can close them."

He did, then opened them again. "Sky Maiden was my mother's Indian name. After she married my father, she was Sky Maiden Sierra. She never took an Anglo name."

Deborah wondered why his statement sounded like a challenge. "Think of how interesting your life would have been if you were Phoenix Maiden Sierra. You could have had some terrific fights at recess."

"I had those anyway." He paused, then said pointedly, "I'm half Indian, Deborah."

"I'm Bulgarian on my mother's side, and Bulgarian, English, and Irish on my father's side."

He frowned in puzzlement. "Why are you telling me this?"

"I thought we were exchanging our lineages."

"I was telling you mine, because it makes a difference to some people."

She knew what it was like to be different, to be made to feel set apart. "I'm not some people. I am a doctor, however, and you still need to get some sleep."

"You aren't leaving, are you?"

She shook her head. "Not yet. I want to check your pupil reaction again in two hours."

"This is getting exciting, Deb," he drawled.

Chuckling, she placed her hand over his eyes. "Go back to sleep."

His fingers closed around her hand, and he drew it down to his chest. "Why don't you join me?"

His offer was tempting. It shouldn't be, but it was. "No thanks."

"You're losing sleep because of me. That's above and beyond the call of duty, Doc. You need to get some rest too."

"I didn't bump my head. I'm also used to getting by without much sleep, so you don't need to feel guilty on my account."

Pulling her hand out from under his, she stood up. "Go back to sleep."

"That sounds like an order."

"Whatever it takes." She tightened her grip on the flashlight to keep from smoothing her fingers over the frown lines around his eyes. "Be sensible, Phoenix. You're exhausted, and you still have a headache."

"How do you know?"

"I can see it in your eyes."

His expression became fierce, which made her wonder if he resented her being able to read him so accurately.

"I'd rather talk to you than sleep," he said, but his

statement lost some of its strength when he followed it with a yawn.

She bit her lip to keep from smiling. "I know," she said soothingly, giving in to temptation and brushing fingertips across his forehead. "It's for your own good, Phoenix. I'm not going anywhere."

His chest rose and fell as he took a deep breath. "That feels great."

Because he seemed to enjoy it, she continued to brush her fingers over his forehead, letting them trail into his hair.

His eyes closed, and his breathing slowed.

A few minutes later she turned off the light.

He didn't give her any problems when she shook him awake at twelve o'clock. He opened his eyes just long enough for her to shine the light in them, mumbled her name instead of his own, then went back to sleep. She gazed longingly at the wide bed and his long body sprawled across it. Both the bed and Phoenix were looking more inviting as the night progressed.

Even though his pupil responses were normal, she still planned on awakening him one more time at two in the morning. Then she would call a cab and go home.

At one-thirty, Deborah staggered down the hall to the closed door at the far end, hoping to find a guest room with a decent bed. Trying to get comfortable on the curved living-room sofa—which had been designed for active seduction, not restful slumber—had been as futile as trying to find silence at a pep rally. Pressing one hand to the small of her back to rub her stiff muscles, she turned the knob and opened the door to—she hoped—the guest bedroom.

The hall light didn't illuminate the room well, and Deborah couldn't see anything that resembled a bed.

Or any bedroom furniture of any kind. Reaching inside the door, she smoothed her hand over the wall, searching for a light switch. When she found it, she flicked it and stepped into the room.

No, there wasn't any bedroom furniture. Instead she saw cabinets, a sprawling rack of assorted chisels and other tools, and a long worktable stretching against the far wall. Extension lamps were clamped onto the table, and a piece of heavy felt was spread over it. A number of small objects lay on top of it. After seeing the tiny scars on Phoenix's fingers, she wasn't at all surprised to see the wood-carving tools. What amazed her was the amount of equipment. It was staggering. A lot of time and effort had gone into this workroom, taking it way beyond a hobby of occasionally whittling on a stick.

She realized something felt odd under her bare feet and looked down. A wall-to-wall sheet of white canvas had been tacked down to protect the floor and to catch wood shavings. Unable to resist, she crossed the room to a sheet-covered platform set across two sawhorse frames.

Keeping in mind what curiosity did to the cat, she gave in to temptation and reached for the edge of the white cloth. Carefully lifting a corner of the sheet, she peered underneath, then froze in astonishment. Using both hands, she peeled back the sheet in order to see the entire display.

Deborah stared spellbound at the scene in front of her. There were miniature hogans covered in sticks and mud, frames with animal skins spread out on them, looms with closely woven fabric on them. It was an Indian village from long ago, when life was more primitive and beautiful in its simplicity.

She slowly walked around the platform, never taking her eyes off the village. She saw campfires, children, men, women, sheep, horses, trees. Leaning closer, she spotted a tiny bird's nest in one of the trees, complete with eggs inside it. Stepping back, she tried to take in the whole village. It was the most astonishingly beautiful, charming display she'd ever seen. Considering her experiences with the carnival and the traveling she'd done all over the country, that was saying quite a bit.

It was impossible for her to imagine the hours it had taken Phoenix to create the display. She knew she wouldn't have been able to accomplish such incredible beauty in an entire lifetime.

She could have stayed in the workroom for hours examining the display, but the sound of a ticking wall clock reminded her it was time to check on Phoenix.

After she re-covered the Indian village, she gave the workroom one last look, then turned off the light and closed the door behind her. She hadn't found a comfortable bed, but she had discovered an intriguing piece of the puzzle called Phoenix Sierra. It was a discovery she was going to keep to herself, though. The fact that Phoenix had created the Indian village with love and respect revealed more about him than he might want her to see. Keeping his creation tucked away behind a closed door clearly showed he created the carvings for his own benefit, not for public display. If he wanted her to know about his work, he would show it to her. Otherwise, she wouldn't mention it.

Entering his bedroom, she saw he was lying on his side. Sometime during the last two hours he'd unbuttoned his shirt but hadn't removed it. Her gaze slid down his tanned chest, over his flat stomach, and focused briefly on the fastening of his jeans before she looked away. She turned on the lamp on the square table beside the bed. The dark colors of the walls and furnishings gave the room an intimate atmosphere she needed to dispel as much as possible.

Touching his shoulder, she shook him gently. "Phoenix. Wake up for a few minutes."

He made a sound that could have been an assortment of curse words or just general protest. Whatever he was trying to say was unmistakably cranky. His eyes remained closed.

Sitting on the edge of the bed beside his hips, she gave his shoulder another nudge. "You have to open your eyes, Phoenix."

"Why?" he growled, not obeying her request.

"Come on," she coaxed patiently. "Just long enough for me to see your eyes. You know the routine by now. Humor me by doing what I ask, then you can go back to sleep."

Even though his eyes remained closed, he reached out and unerringly clamped his hands around her waist. "We've been doing things your way all night. Now we'll try them my way."

He easily lifted her over him and placed her beside him, then rolled over to face her. Ignoring her sound of protest, he tucked her against his long body, one arm under her, the other across her hips, as he buried his face in the curve of her throat.

He was hard and hot against her, and Deborah felt her head swim. She was shocked to discover one of her hands was clutching his shoulder, holding on, not pushing him away.

"Phoenix, let me up."

His reply was muffled against her throat. "No."

He'd thrown one of his legs over hers, anchoring her firmly to the bed. She should be outraged. She should be yelling at him. She should be threatening him with bodily harm. She wasn't doing any of those things.

Rather than asking herself why she wasn't angry, she slid one hand beneath his open shirt and across the corded muscles of his shoulder. When her fingers feathered through his hair, he made a soft moan of pleasure. She repeated the action, carefully avoiding the area that had come in contact with Belle's window.

It wasn't quite the way the test should be done, but she improvised. "What's my name?"

"Flame," he murmured as he touched her throat with his mouth.

She shivered in response. "Flame?"

"Hmmm. Flame. Fire Woman with hair the color of hot coals."

She didn't know if he was simply rambling in his sleep or was having hallucinations. "Does your head still ache?"

"I ache," he said huskily. "But not that high up."

She closed her eyes hoping to shut out the riot of emotions slashing through her. His hand pressed her hips into his, and she felt his heat and hardness.

She grasped at her profession as though it were a safety line that would save her from drowning in sensation. "What's your name?"

"Idiot."

She choked back a laugh. "Why?"

He opened his eyes and looked at her, his mouth only inches from hers. "Because you've been here all night, and I've been sleeping. I'd call that a royal waste of time, not to mention dumb on my part."

He shifted onto his back, bringing her with him. One arm held her securely, the other supported his head so the sore spot wasn't pressing into the pillow. The room was quiet and dark and intimate.

"That's not being an idiot," she said. She fought the urge to kiss his neck. "That's being smart. You were exhausted."

"That's a lousy excuse. I finally have you in my apartment, and I conk out. But I've recovered, and I have you in my bed now, so I guess I'm not as dumb as I thought."

"I'm here to wake you up every two hours and look at your eyes and ask you your name, not to sleep with you."

"Gee, Doc. You're a real fun date."

"This isn't a date."

For a moment he didn't say anything. Tension stiffened his arms briefly before he forced them to relax. "What is this then?" he asked in a strangely pensive tone.

She sighed and laid her head on his shoulder, fatigue and confusion undermining her common sense. "I was hoping you knew."

His fingers delved through her long hair, lifting it, then letting it fall. "Well, I don't. I guess we'll just have to wait and see what develops."

"We aren't rolls of film. We don't have to do anything we don't want to do, and I don't want to get involved with you."

A low chuckle rumbled through his chest. "Flame, you're in a man's bed at two o'clock in the morning. It'd say that's a little involved."

So would she, Deborah admitted to herself.

The comfortable bed, his warmth, and his gentle caresses combined to weaken her resistance. She should get off the bed, move away from his intoxicating touch, and let him rest. Lying on the bed with him was unprofessional and incredibly stupid, though not because she was afraid he would take advantage of the situation. She was more afraid of how devastated she would feel if he didn't.

Disgusted with her contradictory feelings, she started to roll away from him to prove he was wrong. Or to prove to herself she could.

His arm tightened instantly around her. "Where are you going?"

"Home."

He wouldn't let her go. "Stay. I'll take you home in the morning." He pressed her head back onto his shoulder. "You've been taking care of me all night. Now it's my turn."

Her bones seemed to melt into the mattress as he began to stroke her back. "I'm supposed to be taking care of you."

"Why?"

Even though his voice was low, almost a whisper, she thought she detected a note of bewilderment in it. "I'm a doctor, remember? We do stuff like that."

"Dr. Justin stitched up my arm. But it was Deborah who drove my truck and stayed with me. I want to know why you would lose sleep over a man you don't want to get involved with. Does it have something to do with what you said in the emergency room?"

"What did I say?"

"That it might be your fault I'd been henpecked."

"Oh, that."

"Yeah, that."

She knew him well enough to realize he wouldn't be satisfied with a vague answer. "Shortly after I met Belle, she told me about some of the practical jokes she's had to put up with, and I told her about some of the things med students I knew used to do to one another. One of them involved a carload of frogs from one of the labs. Belle improvised with a chicken. I didn't connect her with the incident until you mentioned her name and that she was dating a policeman."

"So you're here because you feel guilty?"

His body had stiffened against her, and she'd heard the reproach in his voice. "I would have felt guilty if I had put the chicken in your car myself. I didn't. I did feel responsible for giving Belle the general idea, but that isn't why I'm here."

He didn't ask again why she was there. Somehow his silence did that for him, and she felt a sudden anger race through her. Anger with him, with herself, with the situation, with all the unanswered questions and the confusion deep inside her.

Rising up on her elbow, she stared down at him. The light from the hallway allowed her to see his face, but he wasn't allowing her to see what he was thinking. She recognized a well-armed defense when she saw one.

"I don't know what's going on between us," she said. Her voice cracked on the last word as she bit it off. She took a deep breath and added, "I know why I'm in your apartment but not why I'm in your bed."

He shifted her onto her back, partially covering her with his body. His scarred fingers slid through her hair as he brought his hands up to frame her face. "It seems there's two of us who don't know why in hell we're attracted to each other—except for this." He lowered his head. "I understand this."

As before, he kissed her with complete confidence and command, no hesitation. Deborah felt as though she'd stepped off a high cliff without having taken the long, slow walk to the top. Preliminary moves toward seduction weren't necessary. Sweet words and soft music hadn't been needed. All it took was a touch, a taste, and they were deep into passion and desire.

Phoenix thought he would explode when he felt her legs part as he positioned himself over her. He'd never fit a woman so well, so perfectly, and his mind spun with the implications. He murmured her name and deepened the assault on her mouth, taking her with him into uncharted territory.

Deborah vaguely felt him tug her shirt from her waistband; then roughened fingertips were gliding over her skin. The lace covering her breasts became a sensual barrier between her sensitive flesh and his provocative touch.

She was allowing him to do too much, too soon. This man was practically a stranger, and she was in his bed, his hands caressing her, his aroused body molded to hers.

And she was aching for more.

Another taste of her and he would stop, Phoenix told himself. Her breasts were firm and soft under the lace. Her skin was like hot silk, searing his fingers yet soothing his need to feel her sultry curves.

He sucked in his breath, and the muscles of his stomach trembled when he felt her fingers slide down his torso and pause at the fastener of his jeans. Bringing his hand down between them, he gently pried her fingers away, then pressed the palm of her hand to the front of his jeans. When her fingers stroked the hard ridge against the zipper, he groaned deep in his throat.

With what little control he could find, he rolled away from her, allowing himself to hold on to her hand but not trusting himself to have more of her. His body was aching, but he knew he couldn't take her tonight. Even while his body cursed him, his mind was commending him. He could have her tonight, but he might then be forfeiting tomorrow with her.

For the first time in his life he wanted a tomorrow with a woman.

And that scared the hell out of him.

He heard her take a deep, ragged breath, then she spoke. "You were saying something about not knowing what you were doing?"

He started to laugh. Rolling onto his side, he brought their entwined hands up to his chest. "You have one helluva beside manner, Doc."

Her smile was a little shaky. "Since this seems to be the time of night for questions, I have one more."

A corner of his mouth curved upward. "Just one? I can think of about a dozen at the moment."

Her hair shifted on his pillow when she turned her head to meet his dark gaze. "Why did you stop?"

He started to speak, then hesitated. Shaking his head, he murmured, "I can't do it. I was going to come out with a slick comment that would make a joke out of the last few minutes. It's what I would have done before."

"Before what?"

"Before I met you." He smiled at the way her eyes widened in shock. "You have a bad effect on me. I feel this disgusting need to be honest with you." He stroked his thumb across her bottom lip. "I could give you the old excuse of having a headache, although it's usually the woman who hands that one out."

"In your case it would be true."

"No, the headache's gone. If things were different, I would have taken your clothes off and made love to you until neither one of us could walk."

Deborah swallowed with difficulty. "But you're not going to."

"Not this time. One-night stands are all I've ever offered a woman before. I want more than one night with you."

She recognized the wary expression in his eyes. "And you don't like wanting more," she said astutely.

"No." He stroked his thumb over her moist lips, and his tender touch was at odds with his stark answer. "I don't like wanting you this much."

She should be relieved he felt the same way she did. So why did his words hurt so much? she wondered helplessly.

"You've wrapped things up nicely," she said. "Now I'll put the bow on it. I don't want to get involved with you or anyone else at this point in my life, so it looks like we're both in the clear."

He uttered a succinct two-syllable word straight out of a barnyard, though he softened it with a smile. "The hell we are. If this is being in the clear, why is it that I can't imagine being with another woman? That's never happened to me before. Now when I think of touching a woman, making love to a woman, it's you."

"That's because I'm here. Let me go home, then you won't have to think about me at all. Out of sight, out of mind."

"That's isn't how it's worked so far, Flame. You're all I've thought about since I saw you in the emergency room. Being with the real thing instead of the fantasy is much better, believe me."

She was too tired to argue. Sighing heavily, she remained still for a moment, gathering strength to get off the comfortable bed. When she thought she just might make it to a vertical position, she tried to pull her hand free from his.

His fingers tightened around hers. "No. Don't leave. It's too late for you to go home now."

It was too late for a lot of reasons, she thought as she stopped resisting his hold. "Phoenix, I'm tired. I need to go home."

"All you have to do is close your mouth and those beautiful eyes and go to sleep."

"I thought we just decided I wasn't sleeping with you."

He pulled her into his arms and pressed her head onto his shoulder. "I don't think sleeping had anything to do with our recent conversation." His sigh had a distinct martyred edge to it. "Lord, I don't believe this. I'm actually going to sleep with you."

It was incredible, but she felt like laughing. That was one of the things she found irresistible about him, his ability to make her find humor in any situation. Especially this one.

"Phoenix?"

"Don't push your luck, Doc. I'm barely hanging on to my good intentions as it is. Let's discuss this in the morning, when my head doesn't feel like it's wrapped in cobwebs and my body doesn't feel like it's been lying on the finish line of the Indianapolis Speedway."

"This is crazy."

"I agree, but the alternative is both of us trying to get some sleep alone. We'll figure out what we're going to do about this later."

She sighed. "Good night, Phoenix."

He made a sound that could only be called a grunt.

Smiling, she sank into his warmth and closed her eyes.

She rationalized her staying in his bed by telling herself there wouldn't be any harm in sleeping in Phoenix's arms. If she insisted on going home, he would insist on driving her. He needed to rest. She was staying for the sake of his health. And that was pure baloney.

The only sound was the faint ticking of the alarm clock on the bedside table. The warm intimacy of the room and the darkness made her feel as though they were the only people in the world.

It was a lovely thought. And the last one she had until dawn.

Phoenix awoke swearing and automatically swung an arm toward his alarm clock. The scent of jasmine floated in the air, and he smiled. Rolling over, his eyes still closed, he reached for Deborah. All he found was a cool sheet.

Opening his eyes, he took in the rumpled sheet and blanket and the empty space beside him.

"Dammit, Deborah," he said aloud.

Five

Four hours into her shift at the hospital, Deborah was writing up a prescription at the center counter, when one of the nurses plopped a package down in front of her.

"What's this, Sandy?" she asked, looking up.

"Someone left this for you at reception."

Deborah pushed it aside and signed her name at the bottom of the prescription. She handed it and the medical record to the nurse who was waiting for it.

She was reaching for another medical record, when Sandy asked, "Aren't you going to open the package?"

"I will—later."

"Aren't you even curious?" Her voice vibrated with amazement.

Deborah glanced at her, a smile replacing the impatient frown. "Are you hoping another grateful patient dropped off a batch of chocolate-chip cookies like last week?"

"It would be nice, but I don't think this is cookies." Sandy tapped the brown-paper-wrapped package.

"This has *Personal* written on it twice, your name without M.D. behind it, and a colored drawing of some kind of bird surrounded by flames."

That got Deborah's attention and drew some of the other staff over to the counter as well. Gifts from discharged patients were a fairly common occurrence and were usually shared among the staff, especially if they happened to be food. Unusual items were prized for their gossip value. They were less fattening and much more interesting.

Turning the package over, Deborah saw the sketch of a mythical bird rising up from fire. A phoenix rising from the ashes. Oh, Lord, she groaned silently. Knowing who had sent the package, she wondered if something was going to spring out of it when she opened it. And with so many curious onlookers, she was going to have to open it now.

She carefully peeled back the tape and unfolded the paper. Sandy didn't bother hiding her disappointment and said aloud what everyone else was thinking.

"A book? An old book at that. I thought it was a box of candy."

"You mean you were hoping it was a box of candy," one of the other nurses teased.

Deborah turned the book so she could read the spine. "'*Good Manners and Proper Etiquette*,'" she read aloud.

Opening the book carefully, just in case it held more than pages, she saw something had been written in faded blue ink on the inside of the cover. *Property of Sky Maiden.* She stared at the neat script. The book had belonged to Phoenix's mother. He'd sent his mother's book to her. If this was his idea of a practical joke, she failed to see the humor. Why in the world would he do such a thing?

"What kind of gift is a book on etiquette?" another nurse asked. "Who's it from?"

"It doesn't say," she answered, closing the book before anyone could read the inscription.

Although she already knew who sent it, Deborah went through the motions of looking for a card. As she leafed through the pages, she found a sheet of paper inserted in the middle of the book. This was not the time to take a closer look at whatever Phoenix had put inside. The hospital grapevine would have a ball with Dr. Justin receiving a note in a book on etiquette from a man.

"Evidently, one of my patients thinks I need work on my manners," she said.

Bill Freeden, one of the other doctors, chuckled. "The only complaint I have about your manners is when it comes to turning down my generous offers to take you away from all this. All you ever say is no. Not even 'No, thank you, you handsome devil.' Just a heartless, blunt *no*."

As she folded up the brown wrapping paper, Deborah removed the piece of paper from the book and slipped it into her coat pocket. "Wait until I've had a chance to read the book. Then I'll be able to turn you down more politely."

Grinning at her, he accepted a medical folder from Sandy and headed toward one of the cubicles to attend to a patient.

With assorted mutterings and conjecture the group broke up, and they all went back to their various duties. The faint wail of a siren in the distance had everyone moving a little faster to prepare for the emergency about to arrive. Deborah slid the book and wrapping paper into the cubbyhole with her name on it. It would be a while before she could read the note Phoenix had sent.

It was a full two hours before she was able to go into the staff lounge for a cup of coffee. She kicked off her shoes and sank down onto the sagging stuffed chair in a corner of the lounge. Ignoring Bill stretched out on the couch, she took a sip of coffee and cringed at the bitter taste. She set the cup on the littered table next to the chair, then eased the note out of her pocket, and unfolding it carefully so it didn't rustle. She wasn't ready for Bill or anyone else in the hospital to find anything to gossip about concerning her private life.

Although she'd never seen his handwriting before, she could have guessed the bold script would belong to Phoenix.

He'd written, *My mother drummed good manners in my brother and me whether we wanted them or not. One part of social conduct she didn't mention was the proper way for a woman to behave after spending the night in a man's bed. For future reference, look on page 59.*

It wasn't signed except for a smaller sketch of the mythical bird in the flames.

Gently, as though the note were made of spun-glass, she folded it again, then simply held it in her hand. She hadn't brought the book in with her, so the part he wanted her to read would have to wait until later.

The man was going to drive her crazy. He wasn't taking any detours or side trips. He was driving her straight to the brink of infatuation. A woman wouldn't know what to expect from him, but she certainly wouldn't be bored.

She slid the note back into her pocket, and glanced at her watch as she stood up. With any luck, she would be kept so busy the rest of her shift, she wouldn't have time to think about Phoenix and all the ways he drove her nuts.

Because of a late staff meeting, Deborah didn't leave the hospital until ten-thirty that night. As she drove home, the book Phoenix had sent her sat on the seat next to her, along with her shoes, which she'd taken off before driving home.

She half expected to see his large black Bronco parked in front of her town house, and was more than half-disappointed that it wasn't there. Once inside, she purposely took her time changing out of her work clothes, taking a shower, and slipping into a tracksuit that had seen more miles than Belle's car.

After she'd heated water for a cup of tea and had watered the pathetic African violets on her kitchen windowsill, she pushed the Rewind button on her answering machine for messages.

The first one was from her mother. "Hi, Debbie. How are you? Why aren't you ever home, so I don't have to talk to this darn machine? We still plan on being in Richmond next week. See you then."

As if her life hadn't enough turbulence, she thought, the arrival of Krakor and Ellie Justin would certainly stir things up nicely.

Her next two messages were dial tones, indicating hang-ups, then a salesman extolled the virtues of vinyl siding. There was no message from Phoenix. She reset the machine and took her cup of tea with her into her bedroom. Curling up in bed, she leaned against the headboard and reached for the book Phoenix had given her. She turned the yellowed pages until she'd found page 59. Added to the end of a chapter was a handwritten paragraph:

The appropriate sleep-over etiquette begins with waking the guest with a kiss in the morning, followed by romantic phrases and frequent touching. Agreement can be made beforehand or upon waking as to who makes coffee, who gets the shower first (if not shared), and discussion can commence for the next meeting. The most important part, and quite necessary, is that both parties be there and not disappear some time during the night. This is extremely rude behavior and not acceptable.

The last sentence was underlined.

Deborah closed the book. So he was miffed because she'd left while he was asleep. She'd tried to save them both another discussion that would lead nowhere.

Whom was she trying to kid? She'd left before he'd awakened and started to make love to her again. She hadn't trusted herself enough to stop him. Not when it was what she wanted too. So she'd run. And she'd keep on running.

She trailed a finger over the old book and thought about the woman who had read it years ago. Phoenix had kept the book because of sentimental value, and his property should be returned to him. Now all she had to do was decide how she was going to do that.

The thudding sound of Belle's stereo at full throttle vibrated through the walls, indicating her neighbor was still awake. Then she heard several loud, hammering noises on the wall between the two town houses. Belle was definitely awake and making sure everyone else would be too.

Deborah grabbed the book and left her bedroom.

Belle finally came to the door after Deborah kept her finger on the doorbell for a full minute. When Belle opened the door and saw who it was, she instantly apologized. "Geez, I'm sorry, Deborah. I didn't think about the time. Did my hammering wake you up?"

"I'm not here about the noise. Can I talk to you for a minute?"

"Sure." Belle stepped aside and opened the door farther. "Can I get you something to drink?"

"No. Thanks anyway. I have a favor I'd like you to do for me."

"If I can do it, it's yours. Why don't you sit down and tell me what it is."

It was easier to get through the living room now that some of the boxes had been emptied. Deborah perched on the couch where Phoenix had sat. Lord, was it only yesterday? she thought.

She held up the book, "Would you give this back to Phoenix when you go to work tomorrow?"

Puzzled, Belle glanced at the book. "Why don't you give it to him yourself?"

"It's complicated," she said, feeling as though she had made the understatement of the year. "Would you just give it to him please?"

"Is it his book?"

"He sent it to me at the hospital, but it belonged to his mother, and I think he should have it back."

Belle pursed her lips for a few seconds, then shook her head. "No, I don't think so. He takes a lot of guff from me at the office, but even I draw the line at interfering with his love life. He obviously wanted you to have it, or he wouldn't have sent it to you."

Deborah didn't press the issue. It had been a stupid idea she'd come up with out of desperation. "Forget it. It doesn't matter. What were you hammering?"

Belle let her get by with the change of subject, and showed her the small shelf unit she'd been about to put up on the wall. Since she was there, Deborah held one end of the shelf while Belle positioned it over the nails she'd hammered in the wall earlier. Then, book in hand, Deborah went back home.

The following day, while she was on duty at the hospital, she received another surprise from Phoenix. This time it was a large box of cactus candy, spines and all. For some odd reason, none of the staff seemed all that eager to try it, until one brave soul sampled a piece and declared it delicious.

The note inside—which she'd snatched out of the box so the nurses wouldn't see it—read: *These reminded me of you. Prickly yet sweet.*

Stuffing the note into her coat pocket, she left the box on the counter and went to the pay phone outside the emergency room.

When she heard Belle's familiar voice answer, "Sierra Construction," she said, "Belle, this is Deborah. Could I speak to Phoenix, please?"

"He's in the warehouse." Before Deborah could tell her she'd call back, Belle added, "I'll put you through. Hang on."

Deborah's fingers tightened around the phone when she heard a man's voice above the noise of a power saw in the background. "Yeah?"

Feeling foolish, she raised her voice to be heard over the racket. "Is Phoenix Sierra there?"

"Just a sec." Whoever had answered the phone yelled, "Hey, boss. Some dame wants ya on the phone."

Leaning against the wall, Deborah looked up and saw several interested glances being sent her way by some of the people seated in the waiting room. She changed position so she was facing the other way. Now she was receiving the curious glances from the two women behind the reception desk.

She was about ready to hang up, when she heard Phoenix come on the line. "Deborah?"

"Yes." How had he known it was her?

"It took you long enough."

She hadn't the faintest idea what he was thinking about, which wasn't all that new. "I want you to stop sending things to me at the hospital."

"All right. What time do you get off work?"

"Eight o'clock. What has that got to do with anything? Just stop—"

"Your place. Eight-thirty."

He hung up. She did the same, being very careful not to slam down the receiver. It would give her the greatest satisfaction, but she was creating enough curiosity as it was.

It wasn't possible for her to leave the hospital at eight o'clock. Because of a car accident involving a family of five and an elderly couple, she'd been needed to assist with all the serious injuries.

It was closer to nine than eight when she finally slid into her car. She grasped the wheel tightly, took a deep breath, and tried to put the last hour into perspective. Regardless of the skill of the medical staff and the modern technology at their disposal, they hadn't been able to save two of the car-crash victims. One was a three-year-old child, the other an eighty-two-year-old woman.

No matter how hard doctors fought to save lives, sometimes they lost the battle. She knew that; she accepted it because it was a fact of life. But she would never get used to it.

She took off her shoes and barely resisted the urge to throw them out the window. It would have been the next-best thing to hitting something, but neither gesture would ease the pain inside her.

She started the engine, and turned on the radio to fill the car with sound. After lowering the windows to let in the cool night air, she backed out of the parking space.

Phoenix leaned against the tree in front of Deborah's town house, his arms crossed over his chest, and watched her car turn into her driveway. The headlights from her car were enough for him to see her expression as she stared at his Bronco parked ahead of hers.

He shook his head in bemusement. She'd forgotten about him. For the last thirty minutes his anger had been simmering at the thought of her standing him up. Discovering he had slipped her mind entirely did not improve his temper.

Until he saw her face just before she leaned forward and rested her forehead on her hands, still gripping the steering wheel.

In less than a minute he was yanking open her car door and reaching for her. Her head jerked up and around when his hand closed over her arm. He saw the surprise in her eyes, and the haunting devastation. He knew the cause of the first but not the second.

He pulled her into his arms, alarmed when he felt her shaking. He drew her closer. After a moment's hesitation she melted against him. When her arms slipped around his neck and held him tightly, he felt his throat close with an unfamiliar emotion.

She was wearing white jeans and a halter-style top of some slippery gold material. And her feet were bare as she stood on her toes, on the tops of his boots. Even though she wasn't wearing warm clothing, he didn't think her trembling had anything to do with the cool night air.

He held her until she loosened her hold around his

neck. Smoothing his hand over her back, he murmured, "Better?"

Her breasts moved against his chest as she took a deep breath. "Yes. Sorry."

"Don't apologize. I'm glad I was here. Rough day?"

Bringing her arms down, Deborah let her palms rest on his chest, oddly reassured to feel his heart beating solidly.

"I've had better."

"We'll have to improve on that."

He set her aside and leaned into her car to shut off her lights and take her keys out of the ignition. On the passenger seat were her purse, a crumpled white coat, and her shoes. She wouldn't need the first two, but he scooped up her shoes and locked the car door.

"Put these on," he said, handing the shoes to her.

Since she was only a few yards from her front door, she didn't want to bother. "I don't need them."

"The grass is wet. Put them on."

Arguing would have required more energy than she could muster, so she slipped on her shoes.

Phoenix took her hand and drew her along with him up the driveway past his truck. Instead of going to the front door, though, he headed toward the gate to her backyard.

She followed him without protest, another indication of how bad a day she'd really had. Closing the gate behind them, he led her to the single willow tree that took up a good part of the small yard behind her town house. He brushed aside some of the hanging branches, revealing the blanket he'd spread out near the base of the tree. Her own antique brass lantern glowed softly over the cavelike space made by the hanging branches.

"What's all this?" she asked.

"When you weren't here when I arrived, I had a chance to look around. The lantern was on your patio table. The rest I got out of my truck."

She looked at him. "I would have invited you inside."

"Next time."

She didn't argue that there might not be a next time. She'd lost two battles that night and wasn't up to fighting anymore. She didn't resist when he indicated she should sit down on the blanket. Curling her legs under her, she ran her fingers over the woven fabric, tracing the pattern.

"Is this Sky Maiden's too?" she asked.

"Her mother's. She taught the girls on the reservation how to make authentic Navaho blankets. My mother wasn't very good at it. She could sit for hours and read a book, but she didn't have the patience to weave blankets."

His mention of his mother reading a book reminded her of the one he'd sent to her. "I want to return your mother's book to you. It's in the house."

Sitting down beside her, he reached over for the picnic basket he'd hidden behind the tree. "Did you read the part I pointed out to you?"

"The part you wrote, you mean."

He handed her two glasses, then brought out a plastic jug and filled the glasses. "Whatever. Did you?"

"I read it. It wasn't bad manners that made me leave." She stared down at the glasses as a distinctive aroma drifted up to her. "Apple cider?"

"Hmmm," he murmured as he delved back into the basket. He took out a round tin and set it down beside him.

"Do you usually carry a picnic basket around with you?" she asked.

"Only when one of our clients gives me one. A real estate agent we do renovations for on a regular basis knows I don't drink alcohol, so she toasted the completion of a project we did for her by providing the cider."

"Why don't you drink alcohol?"

His shoulders rose and fell in a casual shrug. "I don't have much tolerance for the stuff. I'd rather make a fool of myself stone sober than when under the influence of firewater."

His comment gave her another piece of the intriguing puzzle of Phoenix Sierra. It also dispelled another preconception of a featherweight playboy.

Changing the subject, she asked, "What's in the tin?"

"My contribution. A surprise." He took one of the glasses from her and clinked the rim against hers. "To better days."

"I'll drink to that." She took a sip, then asked, "Isn't there a saying about an apple a day keeping a doctor away?"

Phoenix smiled at her, enjoying the way the glow from the lantern sparked the amber lights in her eyes. "That's a whole apple. Cider doesn't count 'cause it's an apple that's all mushed up. Cider's supposed to make a doctor relax."

"Well, it's working. This is very good."

He felt a sense of triumph when she smiled. It was a little ragged around the edges, but it was a smile. He couldn't think of anything he wanted more right then but for her to smile.

Unless it was to have her in his arms. Maybe he could have both.

She'd put her glass down and was rubbing her arms as though she was chilled. With one smooth motion he slipped his arm around her waist and settled her between his legs, her back against his chest as he leaned against the trunk of the tree. She held herself stiffly for a few seconds, then relaxed. His intentions had been fairly pure, to act as support for her and to warm her with the heat of his body, but he hadn't considered how having her so close to him would affect him.

His thighs bracketed her hips, and he was reminded of how she'd stood between his legs in the emergency room that first night. He would find it easier to forget his name than to forget how good she'd felt then. And how incredible she felt now.

Needing to find something to keep his mind away from more basic pursuits, he said, "Tell me about your bad day."

Laying her head back on his chest, she looked up into the branches of the tree. The flickering light from the lantern glowed on some of the leaves, while others remained dark and mysterious. She rarely talked about her work, not because she didn't want to, but because there usually wasn't anyone to tell. The peace and tranquillity of the evening and the security of Phoenix's arms made it easy.

So she told him about the car accident and how they hadn't been able to save two patients. She didn't go into the medical details, not because he wouldn't understand but because it didn't matter. Two people had died. That was the result.

Phoenix heard the sadness in her voice and tried to think of some way to make her feel less pain. "Two people didn't make it, but five other people did."

Deborah stared into the darkness beyond the leaves, marveling at what he had said. With one short statement he'd found the essence of the situation and put it into perspective. "You're right. I forgot that." She shifted until she was leaning against his arm and could see his face. "Thank you for reminding me."

"You're welcome."

Because he couldn't resist, he lowered his head and covered her mouth with his. As before, need rose up like a tidal wave, until he wondered if he'd drown in her. As badly as he wanted her, that wasn't why he was there.

Raising his head, he looked down at her. "I kept telling myself I wouldn't do that when I came here tonight."

She ran her tongue over her lips, as if to savor his taste. "Maybe you should stop talking to yourself."

His heart raced at the implication behind her words. With one finger he traced the moisture his mouth had left on hers. "One of us had better keep talking, or I'm going to forget that I'm trying to be a friend right now."

He shifted her so she was leaning against his raised knee, her slight weight on his other thigh. "Tell me why you're working in the emergency room rather than some other part of the hospital where you wouldn't have to put yourself through what you've gone through tonight."

"There isn't any branch of medicine that is safe from death."

"But in the emergency room you're put under consent pressures just by the nature of constant critical situations."

It was a question she'd never had to answer before, simply because no one had ever asked it. "Right now it's where I feel I make a difference. It's like working at the free clinic. I can see the results of my work almost immediately."

"The free clinic? Was that where you were this weekend?"

"I help out there when I can." She glanced down at the round tin he'd taken out of the picnic basket. "I can't stand it. What's in there?"

"Dessert."

She pried his hands loose from her waist so she could reach for the tin. Once she had it in her hand, she leaned back against his chest with a naturalness she wasn't aware of, but he was.

The top was too tight for her to manage, so he helped her. Once it was open, she stared down into the tin. The contents were in shadow, but she could see enough to realize she hadn't the faintest idea what type of dessert would be lumpy and such an odd color.

"What is it?"

He moved his head to one side so he could see her face. "You've never seen popcorn before? What kind of sheltered life have you led?"

"I've never seen purple popcorn before," she said without any trace of regret for having missed that particular thrill.

He reached around her and picked up a single popped kernel. "Try it."

She did. "Good Lord, Phoenix. It tastes like grapes."

He helped himself to some. "That's because it's grape-flavored popcorn."

She made a face. "Apple cider and grape-flavored popcorn. I'm going to have nightmares tonight."

"Then maybe you shouldn't be alone."

He'd spoken so casually while reaching for another handful of popcorn, she didn't at first catch the full impact of what he'd said. When she did, she set the tin down and moved to face him.

Sitting between his knees, she met his gaze. "We can't spend the night together, Phoenix."

"We can. Believe me, I'm more than capable of spending the night in your bed. What I think you mean is you don't want me to."

"It would be a mistake."

He shook his head, his expression suddenly serious. "It would be magic."

She felt her stomach drop and her blood turn to liquid silver, hot and thick and shimmering. "I thought we agreed neither one of us liked one-night stands."

He drew one leg up and rested his forearm over his knee. "How about a long, drawn-out affair, one-on-one, just you and me with temporary exclusive rights?"

She stood up abruptly and wrapped her arms around her middle to stave off the chills skimming over her skin. One minute they were talking about apple cider and grape-flavored popcorn, the next he was suggesting they have an affair. Not even a love affair, just an affair. Purely physical. And temporary.

She heard him stand, then he put his hands on her arms and turned her around to face him.

"You aren't going to try to deny you're attracted to me, are you?" he asked with a hard edge to his voice.

If it weren't for the desire making his eyes even darker than normal, she would wonder if he was making some sort of joke. She knew he was experienced enough to know she was feeling more than casual interest in him.

Somehow, though, she had to make him understand why she wouldn't agree to an affair. "I've worked very hard to make my life less temporary than it was while I was growing up. I could have gone into the family business and moved from town to town, living in a trailer, but I chose to stay in one place and have a career that would be permanent and lasting. I'm attracted to you, Phoenix. More than I want to be, but I'm not the type of woman you want. I would want more from you than you want to give. Having a brief affair wouldn't be the right thing for either of us."

"We've both admitted that we don't know what the hell it is we feel for each other," he argued. "We're never going to find out if we don't see each other."

He was so close, so warm, and so attractive. She could feel her knees weakening as quickly as her resolve. "Seeing each other and sleeping together are two completely different things."

He sighed heavily and drew her into his arms. Bowing his head, he buried his face in her hair. "I should hope so. Let's not talk about sleeping together for a few minutes, okay? I'm trying very hard not to think about what it would be like."

So was she, she admitted silently as she rested her hands on his waist. She'd meant everything she'd said, but her reasons sounded extremely feeble compared to the way he made her feel.

Holding Deborah's warm, vibrant body against his was a sublime torture for Phoenix. He could feel her breathing accelerate and her heart race, and he toyed with the idea of persuading her to change her mind. Her response when he'd kissed her before had been everything he could have wanted, and he knew he could kiss her into submission. But that wasn't the way he wanted her to come to him.

Since when had he got so damn altruistic? he asked himself. The answer came just as quickly as the question. Since he'd met Deborah Justin.

Raising his head, he slid his hands down her arms and stepped away from her. "I think it's time you went inside. You've had a hard day and could use some rest."

The lantern was on the ground behind him and his face was in shadow, making it difficult for Deborah to see the expression in his eyes. All she had to go by was his voice, which was cool and faintly amused, as usual. Apparently, her rejection of his offer hadn't bothered him one way or the other.

She brushed by him. "I'll help you gather up your belongings."

"Dammit, Deborah. Just go inside."

Her head jerked around, her eyes widening at the tension in his voice. His hands were clamped on his waist, his legs stiff and spaced aggressively apart as he stared down at her. Now she could see the muscle in his jaw clench, and she realized he wasn't as unaffected as she'd thought.

To put an end to the pain for both of them, she moved some of the branches out of the way, intending to return to the house. Then she turned to look at him.

"You made it easier for me to deal with the death of two patients tonight, Phoenix. I want to thank you for that."

He dropped his hands, clenching them into fists instead. Muttering something colorful under his breath, he closed the distance between them and clamped his hands down on her shoulders.

"Oh hell," he growled, and covered her mouth with his.

Desire sliced through Phoenix as he sank into the heat of her. He had to at least claim her this way, even though it wasn't going to be enough. His hands and his mouth were the only parts of his body he allowed to touch her. He took her deep and hard with an almost desperate hunger.

Deborah didn't even think of resisting when the pressure of his lips silently urged her to open to him. His mouth sank into hers, searing her senses with shattering heat. She struggled to break the viselike grip of his hands on her shoulders, and made a whimpering sound of frustration when he wouldn't let her closer. Her nails dragged across his shirt, her fingers finally grasping the material, hanging on as though her life depended on it.

Phoenix groaned deep in his throat and fought to control the urge to pull her down under him on the grass. Instead of slaking his desire, the intimate taking of her mouth tormented him with thoughts of how the rest of her would taste.

His breathing was ragged when he raised his head and looked down at her. Sensuality glowed in her eyes as she met his gaze. A man could easily mortgage his soul when a woman looked at him like that, he thought hazily, and never consider the price he would have to pay.

He dropped his hands. "Go inside, Deborah. Go while I can still let you."

Deborah stepped back, one of the branches brushing against her hair. She lifted a hand to keep it from hitting her cheek. Her hand was shaking.

"I meant to ask you," she said, "to stop sending things to the hospital. I wanted to return your mother's book too. I didn't get around to either one."

"I won't send anything else." His smile was mocking. "I sent the book to irritate you enough to phone me. When that didn't work, I sent the candy. It worked. You called."

She hated the flatness in his voice, especially knowing she was causing it. Making him happy would make her miserable, though. That didn't leave a lot of room for either of them to maneuver. So they had to part.

"I'll get your mother's book."

She walked away from him, unable to see clearly until her eyes became adjusted to the darkness. At least she didn't stumble over anything on her way to the front door. It would have been shorter to go into the town house by the patio door, but it was locked. Once inside, she flickered on the hall light. She heard his Bronco start up, but her car was behind his in the drive, so he couldn't leave yet. She went directly into her bedroom where she'd left Sky Maiden's book.

She returned to the front door and opened it, half expecting Phoenix to be on her doorstep. He wasn't. Nor was his truck in the driveway. Then it dawned on her he'd taken the keys out of her car earlier and hadn't returned them to her. He'd simply moved her car and driven away.

Still holding Sky Maiden's book, she walked out to her car and felt above the visor. Her key ring was there. After she locked the car, she went back inside, walking through to the house to the patio door. She turned on the outside light and stepped outside. The lantern had been replaced on the patio table, its wick extinguished and still smoking. The branches of the willow tree wavered slightly in the breeze. There was no blanket, no basket, and no tall man stretched out on the grass. The only sign that the space under the tree had been occupied was where the grass had been flattened by the weight of their bodies.

Waves of reaction shuddered through her as she relived the feel of his mouth on hers. She paced across the patio, wrapping her arms around her waist as though she needed to hold herself together.

Her body ached, her skin was overly sensitive, her breathing erratic.

For someone who had made the right decision in turning down the opportunity to have an affair, she wasn't very happy.

Six

By the weekend Deborah had become resigned to thoughts of Phoenix intruding at odd moments of the day. And night. The nights were worse, when it was dark and quiet and lonely. Instead of easing with time, the need to see Phoenix, to feel his touch, was stronger than ever.

Fate stepped in to help her mind off a man she couldn't have. Due to a booking cancellation, her parents were going to be arriving Saturday, earlier than expected. Since she had promised to help out at the clinic all day, she left a duplicate house key with Belle for her parents to use if they arrived before she returned home. She'd told her father on the phone what he was supposed to do, but that didn't mean he would trot next door as soon as they got there. He could just as easily scout around until he found the clinic and pop in while she was working. It wouldn't be the first time.

She had hoped to get away from the clinic earlier than usual, but there'd been an outbreak of flu in the area, and that kept her and the other doctor busy right up until the time the clinic closed at five o'clock. When she'd first volunteered at the small clinic, which serviced one of the poorest sections of Richmond, she'd had trouble accepting that they turned away patients, simply shut the doors when there were people needing medical treatment. It wasn't possible for the nurses, clerks, and doctors donating their time to work indefinitely, though, and there weren't enough people to man the clinic twenty-four hours a day. She'd reminded herself that she could only do so much and had to learn to let go of what she couldn't change.

That night it was even more difficult to stop seeing patients. People were lined up outside the clinic, ignoring the sign that referred them to the emergency room of the closest hospital. Emergency rooms cost money, which many of them didn't have.

Leaving by the back door, Deborah walked to her car with one of the nurses, Grace Harvey, a cheerful woman in her midfifties.

"I hope Ed's in the mood to cook tonight," Grace said as they reached her car. "All I want to do is sit in my recliner, watch a mindless show on television, and become a vegetable for at least an hour."

"Which vegetable would you like to be?" Deborah asked.

"An onion, or maybe garlic. That way Ed wouldn't be tempted to ask me to go to Paco's tonight."

"What's Paco's?"

"It's a country-western restaurant and bar off Broad Street. Ed has a friend who plays in the band." Grace sighed wistfully. "That man I married can do a mean two-step and still looks darn good in a pair of tight jeans."

"What more could a woman ask for? Sounds like you might end up at Paco's after all."

"Probably. It's what we usually do on a Saturday night. How about you, Dr. Justin? Have you got a hot date at some swanky restaurant? Please say yes so I can think about you having dinner with some gorgeous man at a table with candlelight and a linen tablecloth, while I'm cracking peanut shells and sipping on a long-necked beer."

Deborah chuckled as she shook her head. "I hate to disappoint you, but I don't have a date, hot or otherwise. My parents are in town. We'll probably go out to eat tonight, but I doubt if it will be anywhere fancy."

Grace opened the door of her car and threw her heavy satchel into the passenger seat. "Why don't you bring your folks to Paco's tonight? I know I made it sound tacky, but it's not. We have a lot of fun, and the food isn't too bad."

"I'll keep it in mind. Where did you say this place was?"

Grace told her the location, then got in her car with a final word about hoping to see her that night. Deborah didn't commit herself. A lot depended on whether her parents were even there yet, and how tired they were from traveling. She couldn't remember her father ever being tired, but there was always a first time.

If it were up to her, they would have a quiet dinner, catch up on what had been happening in their lives, then make it an early night. However, with her unpredictable family, it was impossible to make plans and count on carrying them out.

She knew as soon as she turned the corner onto her street that her parents had indeed arrived. A large orange motor home was parked in her driveway. JUSTIN CARNIVAL was printed in large black lettering under a band of windows along the side, and balloons and clown faces in a variety of colors were scattered over the vehicle.

Several neighborhood children were staring at the colorful vehicle. They flicked a glance at her when she parked in her driveway. Since she wasn't nearly as interesting as the unusual house on wheels, the small audience shifted its attention back to the intriguing motor home.

The front door of her town house had been left open, and she could hear her father's booming laughter as she walked up the driveway, followed by her mother's scolding voice. She was surprised to hear her mother warn her father not to break Deborah's good china. Her father juggling her china didn't surprise her. But usually he tossed things around only when he had an audience. That meant she had more company.

As soon as she entered her town house, she saw Belle seated on the couch, with Stan, still in his uniform, beside her. Both were applauding enthusiastically as Krakor Justin juggled four dinner plates in the air. Deborah's mother was seated in an easy chair, a tolerant smile on her face.

One other person was watching her father. Phoenix. He stood near her mother's chair, leaning a shoulder against the wall. Stunned, Deborah stared at him, wondering what in the world he was doing there, especially when she had finally accepted she wouldn't be seeing him again.

Whatever his reason for being there, she wasn't going to ask in front of her parents.

Everyone's attention slid to her when she spoke from the doorway. "Papa, that's my new china."

Her father grinned at her without missing a beat. "Then you'd better not drop any," he said, and tossed a plate in her direction.

Her purse hit the floor with a soft thud as she automatically caught the plate. She returned it across the room as she easily caught the next one sailing toward her. After a few minutes of passing the plate back and forth, she kept the plates, expertly stacking them until all four were held in her hand.

Setting them on a table, she launched herself toward her father and hugged him. He was only a couple of inches taller than she but about a hundred pounds heavier, a little roly-poly man with thinning grayish-red hair and a wide grin.

"How's my baby girl?"

She kissed his cheek. "Relieved you didn't use my lamps."

Sliding out of his embrace, she turned to her mother and leaned over to kiss her. "Hi, Mama. How are you?"

Ellie Justin was deceptively fragile-looking, thin and shorter than Deborah, with glossy hair the same color as her daughter's. She raised her hand to touch Deborah's cheek. "I'm fine, sweetheart." There was still a trace of a European accent in her voice, courtesy of her Bulgarian parents. "Your friends made the mistake of asking your papa what he did for a living."

Taking her mother's hand, Deborah sat on the arm of the chair. "And Papa had to show them."

"Of course. You look tired. I suppose you've been working too hard again."

Krakor walked over to Deborah and brought her back to her feet. "What you need is a bite to eat and a few hours of relaxation. Go change into something pretty, girl. We're all going out to eat at a place your boyfriend suggested."

Deborah glanced at Phoenix, raising a brow at the word "boyfriend." He smiled faintly and shrugged, which she took to mean he wasn't responsible for the conclusion her father had come to about their relationship.

Belle stood up and tugged at Stan's hand. "Stan and I need to change too. Why don't we meet you there?"

She had directed the question to Phoenix, but it was Deborah's father who answered as he ushered Belle and Stan out of the room. "We'll be along just as soon as Deborah is ready."

A few seconds later, Krakor was gently pushing Deborah in the direction of her bedroom. "Mama, why don't you help her while I get better acquainted with her young man?"

Trying to stop her father when he was rushing headlong down the path he'd chosen wasn't easy, but she had to try. "Papa, Phoenix is—"

"Hungry," Phoenix interjected. When he saw she still hesitated, he asked, "Do you have a pair of jeans?"

"Yes, but . . ."

"Wear them. The place we're going is geared toward comfort rather than style."

Deborah bristled. That sounded very much like an order. With her parents there, however, she couldn't say a thing. And he knew it, she realized as she saw the amused expression in his eyes.

Her mother came along with her into her bedroom and sat on the bed. Opening up her closet door, Deborah rummaged through clothing hanging there.

"I like him, Debbie."

"Who, Mama?"

"Don't be difficult, darling. You know exactly who I mean. That tall, dark, handsome man in your living room. I swear he could melt the polar ice cap with those eyes of his. I've heard of bedroom eyes before, but this is the first time I've ever actually seen what that means."

Accustomed to her mother's frank conversation, Deborah continued searching through her clothes. "It isn't what you think, Mama. I've never even been out with him. Was Phoenix at Belle's when you arrived?"

"He called earlier today, and your father answered the phone. I told Krakor to let your machine pick up the call, but you know your father. He couldn't pass up a chance to chat with someone."

Deborah pulled out a pair of jeans and a cotton sweater the color of rich gold. "How did Phoenix get from being on the phone to being in my living room?"

Ellie walked over to the dresser and opened the jewelry box she'd given her daughter on her sixteenth birthday. The tinkling sound of a music box made her smile. "Your father invited him to join us tonight. He'd already asked Belle and her friend the policeman to come along. The more the merrier, as far as Papa is concerned."

"Evidently everyone has agreed with Papa, since they're all coming."

Ellie picked up a chain with a locket in the shape of a heart. "I remember when my grandfather gave me this on my eighth birthday. I wish you could have met him, Debbie. He was such a sweet man, with a white bushy mustache that tickled when he kissed my cheek. Your friends were surprised to hear we own a carnival."

The abrupt change in the subject and her mother's tone had Deborah jerking her head around. "I don't know these people as well as you and Papa think I do."

"And they don't know you at all if you haven't told them about your family."

"I don't blurt out my background the minute I meet someone, Mama. I met Phoenix in the emergency room, and Belle lives next door. I haven't had much time to get to know very many people since I've been here."

"That must change." Closing the jewelry box, Ellie shook her head in disapproval. "You need to do more than work. Starting tonight. Hurry and get ready. I'll be in the other room with your father and your man friend."

Deborah nearly groaned aloud. It had been enough wondering what her father was saying to Phoenix. Now her mother would be joining them. She'd better get out there as quickly as she could, before her parents had time to fill Phoenix in on her life from birth to the present in glowing detail.

She sucked in her breath as she struggled to zip up her jeans. She didn't remember them being quite so tight, but there wasn't time to search out another pair.

She'd tugged on the sweater, shoved her feet into leather boots, and finger-combed her hair as she left her bedroom. When she reached the living room, she stopped and looked around.

The room was empty.

There was only one place they could be. Her father would want to show Phoenix the motor home.

Smiling at her father's predictability, she took her keys out of her purse and tucked them into her pocket, along with her driver's license, a credit card, and some money. Once she'd taken a jacket out of the hall closet, she was as ready as she'd ever be.

She locked her front door and walked toward her parents' home on wheels. With a little prodding, she was able to pry her father and Phoenix from the back of the motor home to the front, so they could get going.

Seated behind her mother, she was too far from Phoenix to ask him why he was there without her parents overhearing them. Besides, her father was keeping Phoenix busy fielding all sorts of questions about his business. For a man who had no permanent home, Krakor Justin was remarkably knowledgeable about the construction business. Deborah didn't find it odd, but Phoenix did. He kept giving her startled glances, which she responded to by smiling vaguely.

Her father, with his usual flair for speed, followed Phoenix's directions, and in less time than it had taken her to change, they arrived.

At Paco's.

She couldn't help chuckling as she accepted Phoenix's hand to help her out of the backseat.

"What's so funny?" he asked.

She shook her head. "Fate," she murmured as she started following her parents.

Phoenix didn't understand what she was talking about, but he didn't ask again. Since speaking to Krakor Justin on the phone earlier, he'd felt as though he'd been swept along on a magic-carpet ride. There was no use getting off now, not when he'd got what he wanted. He was with Deborah.

He'd called her on impulse. Or compulsion. Whatever his reason, he was glad he did. Aside from being with her, he was seeing a side of her he would never have guessed existed. This was Debbie the daughter, not Dr. Justin, or Deborah the potential lover. This Deborah juggled plates, for crying out loud. This Deborah had been raised in a carnival, traveling all over the country for most of her childhood. That was according to her father, who had been more than pleased to tell Phoenix about his daughter.

He was also aware that Deborah was still intent on keeping him at a distance, emotionally and physically. But he wasn't going to allow her to push him away. Not again. He'd had a week of thinking about her every waking minute. Staying away from her hadn't worked to rid him of the need for her. Maybe saturating himself with her would.

Catching up with her just inside the door of Paco's, he clasped his fingers around her arm to keep her by his side. She was with him, whether she realized it or not. They made their way through the crowd to the table Belle and Stan had claimed for them.

"Hey, Stud," one of the waitresses called out to him. "Where have you been keeping yourself?"

"Out of trouble, Clare. How about you?"

Clare winked. "Not me. I'll be with y'all in a sec."

When he held a chair for Deborah, she looked at him quizzically and said, "Stud?"

"She thinks it's funny to call me that because I'm in construction."

Deborah could have told him the waitress had a more fundamental reason for calling him Stud. She also couldn't help noticing the looks on some of the other women's faces when they saw Phoenix. She recognized their expressions, because she'd had similar responses to him: dry-mouthed attraction and genuine female appreciation for a beautiful male form.

Due to the size of the table and the number of chairs pushed around it, she was pressed closer to Phoenix than was comfortable. His thigh was against hers, hard and strong, sending tingles of awareness through her that she tried very hard to conceal.

Her father held court at the table like a king

entertaining his subjects. Belle, especially, was enthralled with the stories that flowed from him like an endless supply of sparkling wine. He laughed harder than anyone when Belle accepted his invitation to use his first name, which came out "Cracker" in the woman's Southern accent.

As in a well-rehearsed play, Deborah and her mother responded to the occasional request to supply a date or a place when he couldn't recall it. Otherwise, the two women calmly ate their meal while the others were held spellbound by the stories of carnival life as, experienced by Krakor.

Phoenix was especially fascinated by the stories, that featured Deborah. Now he understood how she'd learned to drive an eighteen-wheeler and a pile driver. She could run a Ferris wheel, hitch up ponies for a pony ride, make cotton candy, and fill in at any of the game booths when needed. His heart ended up in his throat when Krakor told how she had climbed up the frame of the Ferris wheel one time, because a child had become frightened when the mechanism broke down temporarily. She'd stayed at the top comforting the child until one of the mechanics fixed the motor.

She'd been fourteen at the time.

When the remnants of the meal were cleared from the table, Belle and Stan were content to remain there as audience for the showman, but Phoenix didn't want to hear about any other adventures Deborah had had. The thought of her hanging on to thin shafts of metal high above the ground had sent shivers of icy fear down his spine. Even though it was irrational, he needed to feel her in his arms just to reassure himself she was alive and well.

Pushing back his chair, he held out his hand. "Dance with me."

Deborah glanced at him, then at the dance floor, where a number of couples were circling around in a Texas two-step.

Her mother leaned across the table and patted her hand. "You go ahead, Debbie. As soon as your father finishes telling your friends about the tornado of '72, I'm dragging him out onto the dance floor too."

Deborah put her hand in Phoenix's. She could have refused his invitation, but if she did, her mother would fret about her not having any fun.

Phoenix didn't back up to give her room when she stood, so she was only inches away when she warned him. "Don't even think about it."

His eyes widened in surprise. "About what?"

"Calling me Debbie."

He grinned. "I wouldn't think of it."

What he'd been thinking about was kissing her, passionately, thoroughly.

Leading her out onto the dance floor, he placed his right hand on her left shoulder. "Can you two-step, ma'am?" he drawled.

"Can a bird sing?"

He tightened his fingers around her hand and grinned as he led her into the synchronized steps of the western-style dance. "I should have known a woman who can climb Ferris wheels and fill in for a fortune-teller can do a simple dance step."

"Don't believe everything my father tells you. He likes to embroider his stories with fancy details, whether they're true or not."

The music changed to a slower tempo, a song about a man with a broken heart. Phoenix drew her nearer, his gaze never leaving her face.

"You didn't tell me about your unusual background."

He held her so close, Deborah could feel the buckle

of his belt against her stomach. As her body seemed to melt, she dragged her mind back to what he'd said. "You haven't told me about yours," she said defensively.

"I've told you more than I usually tell women I'm interested in. You know about my mother and my brother."

"Why did you tell me about them if it's not something you usually do?"

His mouth twisted into a rueful grimace. "I haven't the faintest idea. I'm doing a lot of things with you I've never done before."

"Like what?"

"Like leaving you when I could have spent the night in your bed. Don't stiffen up. You know it's true. The way you responded when I kissed you kept me awake most of that night. I didn't care for that much. Nor have I liked the fact that no other woman appeals to me. You've ruined me for other women, Flame. You're all I think about morning, noon, and night. What are you going to do about it?"

Since he chose that moment to twirl her around, she had to wait until she was facing him again to answer. "I haven't changed my mind, Phoenix. I don't want an affair."

His eyes seemed even darker in the muted light. "Holding out for a ring and a promise, Debbie?" he asked nastily.

She wanted to hit him. And she would have if they hadn't been in a public place, and if she hadn't been aware of her mother watching them. She had to settle for leaving him on the dance floor.

She'd taken two steps when his arm slid around her waist and halted her. Drawing her back into his arms, he lowered his head to touch her neck with his lips. "I'm sorry," he whispered in her ear. "You've got me so tied up in knots, I don't know what the hell I'm saying or doing."

She closed her eyes, fighting the sensations trilling through her like the passionate strain of violin strings. The emotion in his voice and the tension in his body told her more than his words did. He was as confused about what was growing between them as she was, she realized with astonishment. And he was fighting it for all he was worth.

Placing her hands at his waist, she fell back into step with him, and they blended in with the other dancers circling the floor. The next song was another slow tune, another tale of heartbreak and unrequited love. The rough denim fabric of their jeans created a friction between them with each step they took.

When she heard him suck in his breath, she raised her head to look at him. His gaze burned into her. His name came out in a soft sigh from her lips.

He shook his head. "Don't look at me like that. You're going to be going home with your parents, not me. I'm trying real hard to remember that."

"Let's go back to the table. This isn't doing either one of us any good."

"You go back. I'm going to the bar. I'll join you when I've cooled down enough not to make your father reach for that shotgun he keeps in the back of the motor home."

Since she'd felt his arousal against her while they danced, she didn't need to ask what he was talking about. She nodded and slipped away from him, feeling suddenly chilled when she was no longer pressed against his warmth.

It was a full fifteen minutes before Phoenix rejoined them at the table. The band had taken a brief intermission, so conversation could be carried on without having to yell.

During that time Grace Harvey and her husband had spotted Deborah and stopped at the table to chat with her. After being introduced to her parents and Belle and Stan, they were invited to join them. When Krakor discovered Grace worked with Deborah at the free clinic, he was full of questions about the type of injuries and illnesses they dealt with.

When Phoenix sat down beside Deborah, Krakor was describing one of his own trips to an emergency room. He then listed some of the various injuries workers had suffered in the carnival. He also took full credit for influencing Deborah into becoming a doctor.

"She was the only one who could stomach the sight of blood. I told her to become a doctor and travel with us. Save us all those medical bills. She did one but not the other."

Phoenix leaned toward Deborah. "How much of what he said is true?"

"All of it," keeping her voice low. "Except he didn't mention that he was only kidding when he suggested I become a doctor. He was more surprised than anyone when I entered medical school." She looked over at her father, who had shifted to a story with a happier ending, as far as he was concerned. "We were never in one place long enough for me to attend a regular school, so I did my schoolwork by mail. The one time I did try to go to school was when we were going to be in Bakersfield, California, for a month. I felt like I'd come from a foreign country. I didn't have a thing in common with the other children. I gladly went back to doing my schoolwork by correspondence, until I decided to go to college when I was seventeen. My mother knew I wanted to get away from the life on the road and helped talk my father into letting me go."

"Denver and I spent our summers on a reservation in Arizona and winters in Virginia with my father. After running around barefoot for three months and spending half the time camping out under the stars, we had to turn into respectable sons of a prominent Virginian horse breeder for nine months."

Pleased with the rare glimpse into his past, she smiled. "I bet putting shoes on was the hardest part."

There was no amusement in his responding smile. "The hardest part was trying to figure out which world I fit into, the Indian world or the white world. There's a vast difference between the two."

"Like a carny brat and a city kid. Neither one understands the other."

Phoenix didn't hear any self-pity toward herself or any sympathy for him in her voice. She simply stated what she considered to be the case. And she was right, he realized. Her past had been similar to his own. Neither of them had ever felt they belonged in the different worlds they'd lived in. They'd each made their own niche in life and settled into it.

As if a long row of dominoes had fallen into place, Phoenix understood something else. He and Deborah had successfully made adjustments in order to live their lives the way they wanted. There was no reason they couldn't make one more.

Deborah was watching him, and at the look in his eyes, her breath caught. That look could melt the ice in her soft drink. "Why are you looking at me like that?" she whispered.

"How am I looking at you?"

The answer would be as explosive as the way she was reacting to the heated desire in the depths of his eyes. He was gazing at her as though he wanted to crawl under her skin.

She shuddered with reaction and clasped her arms in defense. "Stop it, Phoenix," she said under her breath. "We've already agreed not to become involved."

He leaned forward and reached for her soft drink, his body camouflaging the movement of his hand under the table. The hand that spread out on her thigh. He smiled as he took a sip from her glass, then returned it to the table.

"I've changed my mind," he said softly as his hand molded to the shape of her thigh.

Her mouth had gone dry. "I haven't."

"Yes, you have. You just don't want to admit it yet. Your father said they're leaving tomorrow afternoon. I'll be at your place at seven, and we'll discuss where we go from here."

He was still holding her glass, and she badly needed something to drink. Guessing her intention, he turned the glass around as she reached for it, so that the part that had touched his lips would now touch hers.

Realizing what he'd done, she considered turning the glass around to drink from another edge. She didn't. Holding his gaze, she brought the glass to her lips and took a sip. Because he was still stroking her thigh, she ran her tongue over her lips, slowly, as though savoring the taste of his lips she'd found on the glass.

He made a dark sensual sound deep in this throat. And removed his hand.

Seven

Sunday night, more than sixty seconds seemed to fill each minute as Deborah waited for Phoenix to arrive. Feeling foolish, she placed her finger on the pulse at her wrist and was not one bit surprised to feel it beating too quickly. She hadn't been this nervous since . . . She'd never been this nervous. Not even when she'd held a scalpel poised over a patient's skin for the first time.

As she paced her living room, she remembered her father's offer to spend the week on the road with them. She could be miles away by now, listening to her father's booming voice as he ran through all the things he had to do when they caught up with the carnival in Norfolk, where it was scheduled to perform for the opening of a shopping center. But when she'd made the decision to see Phoenix that night, she'd known what she was accepting. The attraction that had been simmering between them was about to come to a boil.

She glanced down at herself, feeling ridiculous fretting about her clothes like some insecure teenager expecting her first date. She hadn't changed the cranberry slacks and white V-necked sweater she'd pulled on that morning before fixing breakfast for her parents. The clothes were a little wrinkled, but she refused to change, even though Phoenix wouldn't know what she'd been wearing during the day.

"I'm losing it," she muttered as she sank down on the couch, her legs sprawled out in front of her. "I'm even talking to myself, and he's not due here for another hour. I'll be a blubbering idiot by then."

She nearly jumped out of her skin when the doorbell rang a moment later.

Willing her heart to start beating again, she got up off the couch and walked to the door. She looked through the peephole, then hesitated before opening the door.

"Phoenix," she said with a hint of censure in her voice. "You're an hour early."

"I know," he said roughly. "I couldn't wait any longer."

He didn't wait for her to invite him in either. Placing his hands at her waist, he lifted her out of his way, then stepped in, shut the door, and pulled her into his arms.

His fingers in her hair kept her still for his sudden assault on her mouth. All defenses were down, all pretense swept away. He invaded her mouth and sent her senses reeling with the impact of his undisguised hunger.

She buried her fingers in his glossy black hair and raised up on her toes to press closer to the hard male body she craved. Her case of nerves was gone, replaced by fierce need. She felt the earth shake under her bare feet as his tongue surged into her mouth, meeting and clashing and melding with hers until she thought she would lose her mind.

Denim grazed cotton as he pressed his leg between hers, parting them. The soft whimpering sound she made was almost drowned out by his harsh groan when she arched her hips into his. The weight of his body urged her back against the wall, and she trembled with the sweet ache gathering force deep inside her.

When he broke away from her mouth to bury his face in the curve of her neck, she breathed his name. Right now, this moment, that one word and Phoenix himself were her whole world, all she wanted.

Phoenix's body shook with the passion he heard in her voice when she whispered his name. He raised his head, needing to look at her, to fill himself with the sight of her. Her skin was flushed, her lips moist from his kiss, her eyes glowing embers. With each tortured breath she took, her breasts pushed against his chest. He hated the barriers of clothing separating her flesh from his.

"Deborah," he murmured against the soft, fragrant skin of her throat. "Give me back my mind. You're driving me crazy."

Her fingers tightened in his hair, forcing him to raise his head. "I'm aching. Make it stop."

His arm swept down her back and under her legs. She wrapped her own arms around his neck and closed her eyes as he kissed her while he carried her down the hall to her bedroom.

He lowered her onto the bed and followed her down, unable to be apart from her even for the time it would take to remove his clothes. He slipped his hand under her sweater and caught his breath when he discovered she wasn't wearing anything underneath. Impatient to see her, he tugged her sweater off and threw it onto the floor. After devouring her with his heated gaze, he touched and tasted greedily, her breasts filling his hands, then his mouth.

Deborah's arms were oddly heavy, and her fingers shook as she lifted her hands to the front of his shirt, fumbling with the buttons that suddenly seemed to be her enemy. They wouldn't cooperate when all she wanted was for them to release the body underneath the material.

She made a sound of frustration when the last button refused to budge. "I have other shirts," Phoenix murmured against her lips.

Clutching the two sides of his shirt, she tugged. She grinned with satisfaction when the button flew off and the shirt parted.

With a half-laugh Phoenix shrugged the shirt off, then slowly lowered his chest onto hers. He shuddered and groaned when he felt the softness of her breasts against his heated skin.

Needs escalated. Hands became insatiable. Mouths tasted and savored. Voices murmured, whispered, coaxed, and sighed.

She was sleek and fluid under his hands, exciting him and inciting his desire for more of her. Her scent was like a revelation. And he wanted more. Her mouth was moist and hot. And he needed more.

When she felt his fingers slide under the waistband of her slacks, she willingly raised her hips. When her fingers fumbled with the clasp of his jeans, his stomach clenched and trembled. Neither heard the sound of their clothing sliding off the bed onto the floor.

He wanted to take the time to explore all of her, but he had little control left. He trailed a hand down her stomach and nearly lost his senses when he slipped his fingers inside her. She was moist velvet and hot

satin. The sound of her labored breathing, her exquisite moan, splintered through him.

He held her gaze as he parted her legs and positioned himself between them. The sight of her eyes
shimmering with the heat of her arousal snapped his
control. He surged into her waiting warmth.

"Flame," he groaned as he moved deeply within
her.

Her hands clutched his back, then skimmed over
his hips, his chest, into his hair. She seemed to be
everywhere, enfolding him, enveloping him, deeper
and deeper, until he didn't know where he ended and
she began. Nor did he care. The agony of pleasure
built like a dam about to burst. When he could no
longer hold onto the fevered excitement, he cried out
her name, holding her desperately close as they went
over the edge together.

It seemed like an incredibly long time before Phoenix had the energy to lift his head to look down at
her. Her breathing was as ragged as his, her eyes
closed, her skin flushed with satisfaction. If it were
up to him, he would stay where he was for an
eternity or longer, but he knew he was too heavy for
her.

Reluctantly, regretfully, he roused himself enough
to roll onto his side. But he brought her with him,
unable to bear the loneliness of being separated from
her just yet.

Her hair was damp and mussed and wild around
her face. Her lips were swollen from his kisses, her
skin slick with perspiration. He didn't think he'd ever
seen anyone or anything as beautiful as Deborah
Justin was in his arms.

"Deborah?"

"Hmmm?"

"Is there anything else you wanted to discuss?"

She made a choking sound, part surprise and part amusement. "I can't think of a single thing to say." Then her eyes widened, and she muttered, "Good Lord. I should be shot. No, I take that back. You should be shot."

Her reaction to his lovemaking certainly wasn't the one he'd expected. "Why? You wanted this as much as I did."

"I'm a doctor, dammit. I know better."

He brought his hands up to cup her face. "It wasn't the doctor I made love to, Deborah. It isn't the doctor I want to make love to again."

"Well, the doctor should know better than to have sex without using precautions," she said disgustedly.

He put a finger over her lips. "It wasn't just sex, and we took precautions." He grinned at her look of shock. "You must have been a little preoccupied when I took care of it."

"You took care of it?"

He brushed his lips over hers. "I would never do anything intentionally to hurt you, Deborah. When are you going to understand that and trust me?"

"When I get to know you better, I suppose."

Running his hands down her bare back and over her hips, he murmured, "How much better do you expect to get to know me than this?"

He was talking about physical closeness, Deborah knew, and she was talking about emotional understanding. She wondered if he knew the difference.

She wasn't going to get a chance to think about it, though, or question him about it or anything else, not while he was in her bed with her.

"Let's get to know each other even better," he said.

He rolled onto his back, bringing her with him. His hands cupped her breasts, slid over her hips, framed her face, and brought her mouth down to his. She was swamped with his taste, the feel of his hands rioting over her, then within her.

The irritating, jarring ring of the telephone was followed by a rough growl close to Deborah's ear. Flinging her arm over to the bedside table, she lifted the receiver, accidentally dropped it, then picked it up off the floor. "Sorry," she muttered abstractedly. "Hello."

"Is this Deborah Justin?" a clear, wide-awake male voice asked.

"I think so," she muttered, her eyes still closed. "Who's this?"

"I'm Denver Sierra, Phoenix's brother. Could I speak to him, please?"

She was too groggy to be embarrassed, or to wonder how Phoenix's brother knew Phoenix would be with her.

"Phoenix, it's your brother."

The receiver was taken out of her hand, and she felt him brush his lips over hers just before he spoke into the phone. "Denver, this had better be important. Like a major fire." His irritation changed to concern. "Is he still there? Give me twenty minutes."

He reached across her and hung up the phone, then turned on the light. "Deborah, I have to go."

"What's wrong?"

He swept back the covers and reached for his jeans. "One of the kids we had working for us and another kid tried to steal some equipment tonight. The night watchman caught them, and now they're holding him at knife-point in the warehouse."

Instantly awake, she threw her legs over the side of the bed. "I'm going with you."

"No. You're staying here. I'll be back when I can."

She ignored his refusal and yanked a shirt off a hanger. "If you don't wait for me, I'll just drive myself."

"These kids aren't Beaver Cleaver, Deborah," he argued, shoving his arms through the sleeves of his shirt. "It could go either way. I don't want you to get hurt."

She'd put on a pair of jeans and one shoe and was rummaging around for its mate. "The night watchman or one of the kids could get hurt too. I'm a doctor, Phoenix. I might be needed."

Completely dressed, he came over to her. "Will you do as I say? Stay out of the way until we get these kids under control?"

"I won't interfere, but if someone gets hurt, I think I should be there."

He took her hand and drew her out of the bedroom. He didn't want to leave her at all, much less this way, but he didn't want her in danger either.

Since Stan's car wasn't parked in front of Belle's place, Phoenix used the phone in his Bronco to try to reach the policeman. He wasn't on duty, nor was he home. All Phoenix could do was leave a message at the station and on Stan's answering machine.

When they arrived at Sierra Construction, they could see the lights were on in the warehouse. The large building was set off the road to one side of the smaller building that housed their office. The other buildings were dark except for the outside security lights.

Phoenix pulled in behind his brother's truck, which was parked at the curb. Denver opened the door and got out. As Phoenix opened his own door, he told Deborah, "Stay here."

She stayed and watched Phoenix approach his

brother. Denver was a few inches taller than Phoenix and a little larger in build, but he had the same black hair and similar chiseled features. Even if she hadn't known who they were, she would have guessed the two men were related. Aside from the physical similarities, they had the same stance—proud and arrogant with a distinct air of authority.

After talking with his brother for a few minutes, Phoenix gestured toward his Bronco, then walked quickly toward the warehouse. Deborah started to open her door when she saw he was going alone. Denver reached her before she got out.

"Phoenix wants you to stay here, Deborah," he said.

"Why aren't you going with him?"

"The kid will only talk to Phoenix. The night watchman tried to phone Phoenix, and when he didn't get an answer, he called me. Luckily, Phoenix had given me your phone number, so I knew how to get in touch with him. Phoenix doesn't think the kid is the violent type, but he's scared, so there's no way of knowing what he'll do. If I went in with Phoenix, we can't be sure what might happen to the night watchman."

He stepped up on the running board, and she slid over quickly so he could sit beside her.

"What about what they'll do to Phoenix?" she asked as he closed the door.

"He can handle himself." Denver extended his hand toward her. "Hi, Deborah. As you've probably already guessed, I'm Phoenix's brother, Denver."

She shook his hand. "Why aren't you more worried about him? Phoenix said the kid was threatening the night watchman with a knife. Aren't you supposed to be your brother's keeper or something?"

Denver glanced at the warehouse. "There are only two kids in there. Phoenix doesn't need my help."

Deborah wasn't as convinced as he was. "There are two teenagers and a knife in there. What situation do you consider dangerous enough for you to help him?"

"Six, maybe seven men."

It wasn't so much what he said as the way he said it. He wasn't kidding or even bragging. He was just stating a fact.

"Is that why you haven't called the police?" she asked.

"Like Phoenix, I tried to get a hold of Stan."

"There are other policemen than Stan."

"If we involve them, the kids could get a record. Stan deals with the kids in an unofficial capacity and can handle them as well as Phoenix. He also has the authority of the police force behind him if it's necessary to make an arrest."

Deborah saw a shadow cross one of the warehouse windows but couldn't make out whether it was Phoenix or one of the teenagers. "Why does he do it?"

Denver turned to look at her, smiling slightly. "You mean why does Phoenix spend his nights chasing down runaways and putting them to work during the day?"

"Something like that. I have a feeling it has to do with his own childhood. He told me about living on the reservation for three months in the summer, then trying to adjust to your father's style of living the rest of the time. He said he didn't feel like he belonged in either place."

"He told you that?" Denver shifted on the seat so he could see her better. "Phoenix usually doesn't talk about his childhood. Even with me, and I was there. A long time ago a carpenter who worked for our father helped turn Phoenix around when he was headed for serious trouble because of his temper. Charlie steered Phoenix's anger toward hard work. Phoenix applies the same principle to kids in trouble."

"And the wood carving? Did he learn to do that from the carpenter too?"

"He showed you the village?"

She shook her head, her expression rueful. "When I treated him in the emergency room, I noticed the scars on his fingers. The night I stayed with him after he bumped his head at Belle's, I was looking for a spare bed and found his workroom instead. He doesn't know I've seen it."

"He picked up the wood carving on his own. Don't be hurt that he hasn't shown his work to you. He doesn't share much of himself with very many people."

She leaned forward, her gaze on the warehouse. "This is driving me crazy. He's been in there a long time. What if he's hurt and needs help?"

"You're really worried about him, aren't you?"

She tore her gaze away from the warehouse and met his dark eyes. "I would think you would be too. He's your brother."

He only smiled at her angry attack. "I also know him. He's a very complex man, Deborah. Proud, stubborn, and private. He's also the one man I would want in my corner if I was ever in trouble. The kids he tries to help listen to him because he's been where they've been. He knows how they think, what they're feeling, and how they resent authority. He gets through to them because he understands them. Somehow, the kids sense that and respond to him."

"You had the same childhood he did."

Denver chuckled. "Are you suggesting I'm not as

sensitive as my brother? You may be right. I didn't let a lot of the garbage thrown at us get to me or take it as seriously as he did. I could slough off the cracks about being a half-breed or a paleface. He fought back."

"In some ways he's still fighting," she said quietly.

"Maybe. He's proud of his Indian heritage, but he doesn't cram it down people's throats."

She thought of the miniature Indian village hidden away in his apartment. "I figured that out for myself."

"He keeps his personal feelings pretty close to the chest. He's not an easy person to get to know."

Deborah smiled. "Jumping off a cliff is easy. Climbing it is much harder, but you have a lot more to show for the trip up than you would if you jumped off."

"Meaning?"

"That some destinations are worth taking the time to get there. I'm willing to put in the time."

He reached over and took her hand. "Phoenix told me you were special. It looks like he knows what he's talking about."

"I do."

Both Deborah and Denver looked at the passenger window where Phoenix had suddenly appeared.

Before either of them could speak, he scowled at his brother. "Why are you holding hands with her? You're a married man."

Denver released Deborah's hand and winked at her before turning to meet his brother's glaring eyes. "You told me to take care of her. I was just doing as you asked. Is everything okay?"

Phoenix opened the door and tossed a small pocketknife onto the dashboard. "I sent the kids home. They'll both be reporting to Ralph tomorrow, even though they aren't too happy about it. I told them it was either pound some nails or take a trip to Juvenile Hall."

"And if they don't show up?"

"Then I'll turn them over to Stan, and he can book them. Can you give the night watchman a ride home? One of the kids slashed the tires on his truck just for the fun of it."

"No problem. Does Fred still want to work for us, or do we have to give him hazardous-duty pay?"

"Fred had a great time," Phoenix drawled. "This is the most excitement he's had since he retired from the Marine Corps. Said he wouldn't have missed it for anything."

Denver laughed. Then he leaned over and kissed Deborah on the cheek, ignoring Phoenix's cursing. "I have a feeling we'll be seeing you again real soon," Denver said to her.

"Dammit, Denver." Phoenix took his brother's arm and assisted him out of the truck. "Go kiss your wife and leave Deborah alone."

Denver cuffed him on the arm. "She's all yours. I'll call Courtney from my truck while I'm taking Fred home so she knows everything's all right. You call off Stan so he doesn't come barreling over here. And don't forget you're supposed to be fitted for that costume for Amethyst's party."

"I'm not going, so I don't need a costume."

It was Denver's turn to curse under his breath. "If I have to dress up like something out of *Gone With the Wind*, you do too. So you damn well better get your carcass over to the plantation tomorrow so that blasted designer from Nashville can take your measurements."

"You have to go because Amethyst Rand is your mother-in-law. I don't have to be there."

His brother leaned forward until he was only an inch or so away from Phoenix. "You have to go because you're my brother and part-owner of Sierra Construction. This is Amethyst's party to show off the reconstruction of the mansion, and our company did the work. Think of it as public relations."

"You think of it as public relations while you dress up like Rhett Butler. I'm going to the cabin next weekend."

Denver's jaw clenched. His fists were already balled up and clamped to his hips. Then he threw his arms up in the air in a gesture of defeat. "You talk to him, Deborah," he said, bending down to look through the open door at her. "Maybe he'll listen to you."

She shook her head. "Not me. I don't think Phoenix should go either."

"What!" both men said at the same time, staring at her as though she'd spoken in a foreign language.

"Pretending to be something he isn't isn't Phoenix's style. If he's going to make a fool out of himself, it has to be on his own terms." She grinned at Phoenix. "Going as a Yankee among all the Confederates would be more your style."

For a long moment Denver and Phoenix were speechless. Then Denver murmured, "I'll be damned." Looking at his brother, he added, "She's right."

Groaning loudly, Phoenix started walking around the front of the truck to the driver's side. "Don't tell her that. I'll never hear the end of it."

Laughing, Denver raised his hand in farewell and walked away.

Phoenix opened the door and climbed in behind the wheel. When she started to slide over to give him more room, he wrapped his fingers around her arm to keep her where she was. Without saying a word, he started the engine and pulled away, touching the horn briefly as he passed his brother's truck. As he turned a corner, the knife he'd thrown on the dash skidded across it.

Deborah caught it before it fell off. Holding it in her hand, she asked, "Would the boy have hurt the night watchman if you hadn't stopped him?"

"I doubt it. Terry was more frightened than Fred was. Actually, Terry's hand was shaking so bad he could hardly hold on to the knife, much less use it on Fred."

She opened up one of the blades of the camp-style knife. "There are a number of people who aren't afraid of using knives or guns. We get the results in the emergency room all too often."

Stopping at a traffic light, he took the knife out of her hand. He closed it with a flick of his finger, then reached across her to shove it into the glove compartment. "There's one less casualty in the emergency room tonight."

She studied his profile while he drove, wishing she could see into him with more insight than she'd had so far. "Is that why we do this, Phoenix? To prevent one kid at a time from making mistakes with their lives?"

"Don't make me into something I'm not, Doc. I talk to a few kids, that's all. I put some of them to work to try to teach them that they can get more out of sweating for what they want than from stealing."

"I wonder if all those kids realize how lucky they are to have someone like you to care about them. You should have children of your own, Phoenix. You would be an exceptional father."

"That's one trap I'll never fall into," he said. His voice was hard and inflexible. "There are enough problems in this world without bringing an innocent child into the chaos."

She stared at him. "You don't plan on getting married and having children?"

"No. If marriage is what you're expecting from me after going to bed with me, you may as well know now that I'm not the marrying kind."

Feeling bruised from his harsh tone, she wrapped her pride around her to protect her battered emotions. "I don't expect anything from you, Phoenix, so you can relax."

Even though he hadn't moved away from her, she sensed his withdrawal. A few hours ago they'd been intimately entwined on her bed, as close as two people could possible be physically, but the emotional distance had never been crossed. Now it was widening, and she didn't know what to do about it.

Except give him the space he seemed to need. Maybe by letting him go, she would eventually get closer to him.

When he pulled into her driveway, she wasn't at all surprised when he reached across her to open her door, rather than accompanying her into her house. Her fingers clenched around the handle of her medical bag as she slid across the seat and out of the truck.

The interior light revealed the dark expression in his eyes as she hesitated before closing the door. Since there was nothing to say, she silently shut the door and walked toward her house.

Phoenix waited until she'd unlocked the door and slipped inside. Then, for several more minutes, he sat where he was, his hands gripping the steering wheel, his teeth clenched as he stared at her closed door. Instead of going inside with her, he was sitting there like an idiot remembering the feel of her under his hands, knowing he could have her in his arms again. All he had to do was walk up to her door and ask her to let him in.

Shoving the truck into gear, he backed out of the driveway. Maybe if he drove long enough, far enough, he would be able to forget the hurt and confusion he'd seen in her eyes when she'd looked at him that one last moment.

He knew he was being a bastard by leaving her without an explanation, but he couldn't give her what he didn't have.

Eight

Deborah was thankful for her training in medical school that allowed her to do her job competently while subjugating her personal feelings. So she was fine during her shifts at the hospital. It was when she was alone in her town house that the memories of Phoenix haunted her.

Her childhood experiences had taught her to take each day as it came without expecting far-reaching plans to work out every time. She'd learned there wasn't anything she could do about rainstorms that canceled shows, or epidemics that kept the waiting rooms crowded, or Phoenix Sierra running from a relationship.

On Wednesday, two days after Phoenix had left her in her driveway, she worked late so the doctor who had been scheduled to relieve her could be with his wife while she gave birth to their first child. It was no great sacrifice on her part. It wasn't as though she had anyone waiting for her at home.

At a little after four in the morning, Rob Benedict swept into the emergency room with a wide grin on his face and handing out candy cigars.

"Boy or girl?" Deborah asked as she accepted one of the fake cigars.

"A beautiful bouncy baby boy," he announced, a silly smile on his pale face. "If you planned on hopping up to the nursery to see him, you won't have any trouble recognizing which one is mine. He's the most gorgeous baby in the nursery."

She unbuttoned her white coat, smiling at the proud father. "I'll try to get up to see him later. How's Nancy?"

"She's great. I don't know how I'll be able to repay you for taking over for me, Deb. Whatever you need, whenever you need it, you just ask and it's yours."

"I'll keep that in mind," she said as she removed her stethoscope and put it in her coat pocket. She forced herself to smile, telling herself she was feeling envy only because she was tired, not because she was wishing she could experience the joy and pride she saw in Rob's eyes.

"So fill me in on what's been going on." He glanced around at the cubicles, which for the most part were empty. "A quiet night?"

"Mostly. Waldo, the homeless man who was in here last week with low blood sugar, came in about an hour ago, but we got him stabilized. I have a call into Social Services, and someone's supposed to come and get him."

Rob nodded. "I'll look in on him. Maybe this time he'll accept their help so he won't be back living on the streets again."

The communication system that kept the emergency room connected with rescue services announced an ETA of ten minutes for multiple injuries, including a gunshot wound, two stab wounds, and two fractures.

Deborah met Rob's gaze. "Guess I'd better stick

around for a little longer. It sounds like you could use another pair of hands."

Like a well-oiled machine, the emergency-room staff performed their duties with precision as each patient was brought in. Two uniformed officers accompanied two of the teenagers belonging to a gang and stayed close by in case they were needed. On occasion rival gang members tried to continue their dispute in the emergency room, even when they were badly injured.

After she sent off a fifteen-year-old to X-ray, Deborah stripped off her surgical gloves and pulled on a clean pair as she approached the next gurney. A boy who couldn't have been more than ten watched every move she made with suspicious eyes. A dirty red handkerchief had been wrapped around his upper arm and was blood-soaked.

Before she could ask his name, he said belligerently, "I don't want no woman touching me. I got my rights."

She shrugged. "No problem. As soon as the male doctor is finished with his other patients, I'll send him over to you. It may be a while, though. If you start feeling faint from loss of blood, you'd better give a holler before you pass out. We don't want you breaking any bones when you fall."

His young face became even paler than it had been. "Am I going to die?"

"Since you don't want me to look at your injury, there's no way I can answer your question."

The boy glared at her. "I ain't having no woman doctor."

Behind her, a man said, "She's one of the best, Danny. I'd let her do her stuff if I were you."

Glancing over her shoulder, Deborah saw Phoenix standing next to a policeman.

"Is he one of yours?" she asked coolly.

He nodded abruptly, then ran his fingers through his hair. "There was a small dispute over the ownership of a motorbike."

Deborah raised an eyebrow but didn't comment. For a few seconds she simply looked at him.

He was holding his jacket by one finger over his shoulder. His white T-shirt was soiled, and there was blood on one leg of his jeans.

He looked tired and rough and defensive.

It was a hell of a time to discover she was in love with him.

Feeling light-headed from shock, she looked away, turning her attention to the policeman. "Have you contacted his parents? We need permission before we can treat him."

The policeman consulted a pad of paper in his hand. "Daniel Ortega, age ten. Verbal consent was given over the radio, and the parents are on their way."

The boy groaned, and it wasn't from pain. "Why'd you have to call them? My pa's going to be mad."

Phoenix walked over to the other side of the gurney and proceeded to calm the boy by telling him he would talk to Danny's father. Deborah ignored him and kept her attention on the boy.

"Are you going to let me look at your arm?" she asked.

"I guess," Danny mumbled. "But I don't like it."

"Well, I'm not real excited about having to patch up a young man who should be home in bed instead of playing with knives."

The boy's eyes widened as he looked first at her, then at Phoenix. Deborah concentrated on her work, taking care of Danny's injury, a two-inch slash that she sutured.

When she finished, she ripped off her gloves and

left the cubicle without speaking to Phoenix. Maybe at another time she could act as though everything were normal, but right now she was too tired and too aware of the hopelessness of their situation.

She assisted Rob with one of the other patients, an older boy peppered with buckshot that luckily hadn't been fired at close range. The removal of the small pellets took a lot of time, and she was relieved when it was over. He was the last patient. She could go home now.

Stripping off her soiled coat, she went over to one of the sinks near the nurses' station and washed her hands thoroughly, then splashed water on her face. She held a towel against it for a few seconds, making use of the darkness to rest her eyes. Exhaustion sapped her strength, but she'd been tired before, and she probably would be again. This time, though, she felt an inner fatigue as well. She knew it was because this was the first moment she'd allowed herself to think about her earlier revelation.

She was in love with a man who didn't love her.

When she lowered the towel, Phoenix was standing directly in front of her. His stance was stiff and aggressive, his eyes dark and unfathomable. It would have been easier for her to decipher hiero-glyphics than to read his expression.

"I'll drive you home," he said quietly.

She didn't dare speak for fear her voice would give away too much. She shook her head and looked away.

Stepping around him, she walked over to the nurse's station to check out. Rob called out to her not to forget to see his new baby and thanked her again for taking over for him.

After she'd retrieved her purse, she went out the exit. Forcing one foot in front of the other, she concentrated on the simple act of walking as dawn lightened the sky. When she reached her car, she leaned against the driver's door as she dug into her purse for her keys. She nearly screamed in frustration when she couldn't find them. Facing the front of the car, she started to take the contents out of her purse and set them down on the hood.

"Deborah, let me drive you home."

She looked up to see Phoenix standing beside her. He put her belongings back into her purse, then took possession of her purse and her arm. "You're too exhausted to drive home safely."

She was also too tired to fight him. Or herself. Accepting a crumb when she wanted the whole loaf wasn't the way she faced things, and that was why it was harder than it should have been for her to agree to go with him. Rubbing salt into an open wound was a good description of what she was doing.

She walked beside him to his car, a sleek, sexy-looking Porsche. He opened the door for her, and she sank down onto the leather seat. It occurred to her that she still needed her keys if she was going to get into her town house. Searching for them also gave her something to do when Phoenix joined her in the car. Finally, she found her key ring and stuffed everything back into her purse.

Since Phoenix was just sitting behind the wheel instead of driving, she had no choice except to look at him.

"Why aren't you starting the car?"

"I was waiting for you to get through with your venture into the wonderful world of a woman's purse. I want to talk to you, and I'd like your full attention."

"And I'd like a free trip to the Bahamas. Isn't it too bad we both can't have what we want?" She leaned over and turned the key in the ignition. "You were going to drive me home. So drive."

He drove. Except it wasn't her home he drove to. It was his.

"Phoenix," she said wearily when he parked in front of his apartment building. "I'm too tired to have a major debate with you right now. Just drive me home. All I want to do is go to bed."

"You can do that here." He got out and walked around the car to open her door. When she made no move to get out, he leaned inside and said, "We can do this the easy way or the hard way. Either you walk or I'll carry you. It's your choice."

"I have another one. I'll call a cab."

"That's not one of the options." He grabbed her arm and drew her out of the car. "You're coming up to my place. We'll either go to bed and then talk or the other way around, but you're coming with me. I'm tired of fighting this."

"Fighting what, Phoenix?" she asked bluntly. "I can't see where you're fighting anything. You wanted me. We went to bed. We had sex. You left. What's to fight? You've had everything your way. Taking me to bed was the best in your arsenal of practical jokes, wasn't it? You let me think you cared about me so I'd go to bed with you. Then, when something better came along, like one of your kids in trouble, you dropped me off at the curb and left. No ties. No commitment. No responsibility. You have it all."

Phoenix's jaw clenched. "If this is a joke, why isn't either one of us laughing?"

He took her hand and started walking toward the apartment building with her in tow. He knew this wasn't a good time to have a discussion about their relationship. She was too tired, and he was too hungry for her. That didn't bode well for a calm little chat, but there was no way he was going to take her home and leave her there. Not this time.

When he ushered her into his apartment, he didn't bother turning on any lights. The first rays of the sun were creeping into the living room, providing enough dim light so that they didn't run into the furniture.

Deborah balked when he started down the hallway toward his bedroom. She'd gone along with him through the lobby, into the elevator, and into the apartment. Calmly hopping into his bed as though nothing had happened was where she drew the line.

She jerked her hand from his, nearly breaking her fingers in the process when he resisted. "I'm not sleeping with you," she said. To see his reaction, she added, "You have a guest room. I'll sleep there."

"There's only one bed in my apartment. You're going to sleep in it."

He still wasn't willing to tell her about his wood carving, she thought. She wasn't surprised, but she was disappointed. She wished she could see his face more clearly, but his back was toward the window, the only source of light.

"Then where are you going to sleep?" she asked.

"With you."

"No! The joke's over." She whirled around and stalked to the door. When she reached it, she looked at him over her shoulder. "Someone as experienced with practical jokes as you should know it doesn't work when you try to repeat one with the same person."

He came after her. "This is no damn joke. I've never felt less like laughing."

"Don't do this, Phoenix," she cried when he grasped her shoulders. "Let me go."

Turning her around, he brought her into his arms and buried his face in her hair. "I can't."

She held herself stiffly, as though waiting for the

next blow. Her throat was thick with the tears she wanted to shed but couldn't. He didn't try to kiss her, and for that she was grateful. She bit her lip when she felt his hands smoothing over her back, obviously intending to soothe, not arouse.

She couldn't let down her defenses, though. Not now. It would be too hard to put herself together when he walked away from her again.

Phoenix lifted his head and cupped her face with his hands. "I don't want you to go. We need to be together." She stiffened even more, and he didn't see how that was possible. "I'm not talking about sex. We simply need to be together, to get to know each other better, so there aren't any more misunderstandings."

"Why?"

It was a fair question, he conceded. But he didn't have the answer. At least not the one she might accept. All he could give her was the truth.

"Nothing's working," he admitted. "Nothing's the same since I met you. You've turned my life upside down and inside out, and I don't know what to do about it. Staying away from you isn't working. Maybe being together will. I have to do something, or I'll go out of my mind."

She grasped his wrists and drew his hands down from her face. "What is it you want from me, Phoenix? Do you expect me to jump into bed with you again to make you feel better?"

"Don't," he said roughly. "Don't make what we had together sound so cheap."

"I didn't cheapen it. I didn't walk away as though it never happened. Tell me what you want from me, Phoenix. Am I supposed to come up with some antidote to cure you of whatever it is you think you have? Is what you feel for me some sort of disease?"

He whirled away from her, then turned back. "Dammit, Deborah. If I knew what the hell was the matter with me, don't you think I would do something about it myself? I've never felt like this. I can't eat. I can't sleep. I get into my truck and drive for hours, ending up in places I've never been, trying to find my way out of this panic I feel when I think I'll never see you again. All I think about is you. Kissing you, touching you, sliding into you until the pleasure makes me feel like I'll explode." He ran his fingers through his hair. "So make a diagnosis, Doc. Have I gone crazy, or do I just feel like I have?"

Deborah's heart lurched painfully. She started shaking her head in denial, then stopped. He was pacing back and forth, his hair mussed from his fingers frantically combing through it. His expression seemed tortured, as though he were strung out on a rack.

She stared at him. He loved her! And he didn't even realize it! She thought nothing could be more amazing than discovering she loved him. She was wrong. Phoenix was in love with her! It was the only explanation that made any sense.

All the strength seemed to seep out of her legs. "I need to sit down. Could we have a light on, so I can find the couch without breaking a leg?"

He stopped pacing and returned to her. Sliding one arm behind her back and the other under her knees, he lifted her. "Damn. I keep trying to do the right thing, and I keep fouling up."

She wrapped her arms around his neck. He loved her, she thought again. Why hadn't she realized that before?

He had no trouble finding his way in the dark. As he lowered her onto his bed, he muttered, "You sleep here. I'll sleep on the couch. Later, we'll talk."

She grabbed his arm as he was straightening. He lost his balance and fell across her, flinging his arm out to keep from crushing her.

"Deborah," he said in a tortured voice.

"I've tried sleeping on your couch. It's not very comfortable."

He pushed himself off the bed, then sat down on its edge, eyeing her closely. "What are you saying?"

"Sleep here with me."

He lowered his head to her stomach, resting there, weary and emotionally battered.

She lifted her hand to thread her fingers through his hair in a soothing gesture. As she continued to stroke his hair, she could feel him relax.

Like exhausted warriors, they put down their weapons of words and temporarily set the battle aside.

This time there was no ringing phone to wake them. Nor an alarm clock jangling loudly. Denver didn't come pounding on the door wanting to know why Phoenix hadn't shown up at the office. Closed drapes effectively blocked out the light from the sun that had risen five hours earlier. It was quiet and peaceful in the dark bedroom, and the only sound was the slow breathing of the two occupants of the bed.

Deborah awoke first. Confused for a minute, she blinked several times to try to figure out what was wrong with her bedroom. Warm breath against her neck gave her a clue. She turned her head. Phoenix was asleep next to her. Now she knew what was wrong with her bedroom. This wasn't her bedroom.

Her gaze softened as she soaked in the physical beauty of the man next to her. While he was asleep, his defenses were down completely. His arm rested across her waist; his legs were tangled with hers.

As she took advantage of the opportunity to stare at him unobserved, she wondered if he would have his barriers rigidly in place again when he awoke. Or whether he would allow her to see the man behind the facade.

His lashes were long and curved slightly against his tanned skin. Her gaze lowered to his sensual mouth, then raised to his dark tousled hair. Just looking at him made her want to curl around him and become his in every way possible.

She loved him so much, it frightened her. And he loved her. She was sure of it. Knowing that gave her an edge, but she was at a loss as to what she was going to do with the knowledge.

Lifting her hand to brush his hair back from his forehead, she happened to glance at her watch.

It can't be, she thought. Her watch had to be wrong. It couldn't be eleven o'clock. She looked at the watch again, bringing her wrist closer.

Muttering under her breath, she grabbed the edge of the quilt, preparing to toss it aside. She was stopped by Phoenix's hand tightening at her waist.

"Stay." His voice was husky with sleep.

"It's eleven o'clock in the morning." She slumped back on the pillow. "At least, I hope it's morning and not night."

"Are you as late for work as I am?"

"I'm due at the hospital at one o'clock. I have two hours to dash home and get ready." She leaned on her arm, shifting to face him. "You don't sound very concerned about being late."

"Late for what?" he murmured as he rolled over and covered her body with his.

He consumed her. His callused fingers touched

and stroked and caressed. His mouth was restless and impatient.

Deborah writhed under the sweep of his hands, her skin heating, her breath catching. Like a spark on dry tinder, desire flared into an inferno. Now that she knew what awaited her, she was in a rush to feel it all again. She became immersed in textures; the rough material of his jeans, the smooth cotton of his shirt, the moist heat of his skin, the cool slide of the sheet under her.

She helped him remove her sweater, and her hands were as eager as his to unfasten the clasp of her slacks and pull them and panties down her legs. Her fingers dealt with the snaps of his shirt while he tore at the zipper of his jeans. Like a woman dying of thirst, she drank from his mouth, needing the exquisite feel of his tongue against hers.

She heard the sharp catch of his breath when he dipped his fingers into her, the soft moan of pleasure as he delved into her heated warmth with feathery caresses.

Her body cradled his as he took her mouth with devastating need and slipped into her. She held him tightly as he trembled with the storm overtaking them, clutching him as she met his hunger and responded to it.

He groaned her name, a plea for her to join him as the crest of the storm rose up to consume them. He murmured her name again when she arched up to meet him, and they fell into the maelstrom of shuddering release.

It was some time before Deborah could speak. When she did, she took the biggest gamble of her life.

"Phoenix?"

"Hmmm?" he murmured against her throat.

"I love you."

His reaction was exactly what she expected. He stiffened and started to withdraw from her. She let him.

"I didn't say that to scare you," she said, "although I can see it has. Telling you I love you is a gift that doesn't have to be returned, Phoenix. Whether you want to accept it or not is up to you. It won't change how I feel if you don't want me to love you."

He stared at her long and hard, his expression unreadable, his eyes darker than midnight. "You don't need to say that."

Then he rolled away from her and turned on the light beside the bed.

Blinking against the sudden brightness, Deborah watched him bend down to retrieve his jeans and pull them on. His face was closed, his mouth a defensive tight line.

More than the width of the bed separated them as she got up and reached for her clothing. Gathering them in her arms, she headed for the bathroom across the hall. She stepped into the shower and stood motionless, letting the water sluice over her, her face lifted to the spray. It didn't dissolve the pain. Nothing would. Except Phoenix admitting how he felt about her.

Since that wasn't likely to happen anytime soon, she had better accept it now.

Once she was dressed, she ran her fingers through her hair and ignored her reflection, which showed the strain around her eyes. She pasted a smile on her face and left the bathroom. She was halfway to the living room when she remembered her shoes. She returned to the bedroom—which was empty—and slipped them on. Back in the living room, she picked her purse up from the couch and slung the strap over her shoulder.

"Where are you going?"

She looked up to see Phoenix standing in the kitchen doorway, a cup of coffee in his hand. "I need to go home so I can get ready for my shift at the hospital."

"Have a cup of coffee first, then I'll drive you."

She shook her head. "It's time to leave."

When he didn't move, she took pity on him and slowly walked across the room until she stood in front of him. She touched the side of his face and felt the tautness of his jaw.

"You can't control how I feel, Phoenix. You also don't have to do anything about it. I love you. That's a fact, not a threat, so there's no reason for you to panic. I would like to continue seeing you, sleeping with you, and being with you, but if you would prefer not to see me again, I'll understand."

Going up on her toes, she kissed him, then dropped her hand and walked to the door.

Phoenix never took his gaze off her until she left, then he stared at the door. For the life of him, he couldn't move. He wanted to go after her and make her stay, yet he couldn't take the first step.

He slumped against the doorframe. She loved him. He still found that so hard to believe, so difficult to accept. Then he remembered the surge of emotion he'd felt when she'd first said she loved him. He hadn't realized how badly he wanted to hear those words.

Nor did he understand why she made him so damn mad by letting him off the hook. His fingers tightened on the coffee cup as he thought about her parting words. Where the hell did she get off telling him she would understand if he didn't want to see her again?

He didn't understand a damn thing.

Nine

The following afternoon, Denver slammed open the door of Phoenix's office and marched across the room to the desk. Leaning his hands on the top of the desk, he glared down at his brother.

"I hope you're happy," Denver said. "Belle's in tears, Ralph has threatened to quit, and two subcontractors have called to complain about your mouth. What the hell is wrong with you? You've been going around like a grizzly with a thorn in his paw all week. I never thought I would say this, but I even miss those damn practical jokes you pull on me."

Phoenix threw his pencil down, and sat back in his chair. "Back off, Denver."

"If we want our business to make a profit, I need to shake some sense into you before you and I are the only ones left working here."

"You've always been prone to exaggerate."

"And you've always bent over backward to be fair. Something you haven't been for the last several days. Why?"

Pushing back his chair, Phoenix got to his feet. "I

have some things on my mind, all right? I'll apologize to Belle and Ralph, but not the subcontractors. The plumbers screwed up on that office building, and you know it. If you'd seen the lousy job the dry-wallers did in the Prescott tract home, you would have hollered louder than I did."

Denver straightened up. He examined his brother's face carefully, then asked, "Do you want to talk about it?"

"About what?"

Denver sighed impatiently. "About Deborah. What happened? Did she give you the brush-off?"

Phoenix scowled at him. "Why do you think Deborah is any of your business?"

"She did, didn't she?" Denver said, ignoring Phoenix's question. "Hey, I'm sorry, Phoenix. I really am. I know you care about her."

"She didn't dump me," Phoenix growled, "so keep your sympathy."

"Then what's your problem? And don't tell me you don't have one. I know you better than that."

"You're not going to let go of this, are you?"

Denver shook his head.

Phoenix took several steps away from the desk, then whirled around. Throwing his arms out, he yelled, "She's in love with me. All right? Are you happy now?"

For a few seconds Denver simply stared at his brother. Confusion changed to comprehension. "You make it sound as though that's worse than the bubonic plague."

Phoenix began to pace. "I didn't say it was a bad thing. I just don't know what to do about it."

Denver perched on the edge of the desk and crossed his arms over his chest. "You grab her and run off to the closest minister. That's what you do. What's the problem?"

Phoenix laughed shortly. "You make it sound so easy."

"It is. And speaking as a happily married man, I can highly recommend the institution of marriage. I can't begin to imagine living without Courtney now that I've found her. You're in love with Deborah, so take the next logical step and marry her."

Phoenix returned to his chair and sat down heavily. "I didn't say I was in love with her."

"If you weren't in love with her, you wouldn't be tearing yourself apart like this. You would tip your hat and ride off into the sunset. In the past, when a woman started to get too serious, you dropped her immediately. You haven't dumped Deborah, and you're showing all the symptoms of a man in love."

Phoenix stared at his brother. "You're crazy."

Denver laughed as he headed for the door. "I'm not the one who's crazy. That's you, little brother. That's another symptom of being in love. Sounds like you need a certain doctor for the cure for what ails you." After he opened the door, he added, "Go get her, man. For the sake of our business and your sanity. Put yourself and the rest of us out of your misery and go after her."

He closed the door behind him and Phoenix lowered his head into his hands.

He wanted to go after his brother and yell at him that he was wrong, but he stayed where he was. Because Denver wasn't wrong.

He was in love with Deborah Justin.

He dropped his hands and slumped back in his chair. Feeling raw and exposed, he finally allowed himself to admit he needed someone else to make his life complete.

He loved her.

For a man who had decided to spend his life without strangling himself with emotional ties, it wasn't easy for him to accept that his need for Deborah was greater than his fear of commitment. Even greater was a gut-wrenching terror that he wouldn't be welcome into her life on a permanent basis.

He closed his eyes and shook his head, even though he knew he had found the crux of his insecurity. Ever since he was young, he'd been determined never to let himself become vulnerable to the slings and arrows of prejudice. He'd fought with his fists and, later, with his mind. Gradually, he'd discovered that joking around diffused the tension, and he'd made people laugh with him and not at him.

But deep inside was still that small half-breed boy who had felt different from the other kids and unaccepted by society.

It was time for that boy to grow up. What he had to decide was whether or not he could let Deborah into his life completely, open up all the closed doors he never let people past and allow her to know him. Loving her wasn't going to be enough. He had to trust her, or they didn't stand a chance of having a life together.

He looked down at his hands. His palms were wet from just thinking about revealing his innermost feelings, his fears, his desires, to someone who might reject them—and him. He wiped them on his thighs and reached for the phone.

He hadn't expected to be able to talk to Deborah right away when he called the hospital, so he was surprised when she came on the line. "Hello, Phoenix."

"Hi."

When he didn't say anything else, she asked, "Was there something you wanted?"

You, he wanted to shout. Instead he took the biggest step he'd ever taken in his life. "Can you skip volunteering at the clinic this weekend? There's something I want to show you, and it will take some time."

Her voice was calm as she answered. "All right."

He'd expected questions, maybe even indecision on her part, not instant acceptance. Deciding to push his luck, he asked, "How late will you be working at the hospital today?"

"Until five."

"I want to see you tonight."

"All right," she said again. "I should be home by five-thirty."

"I'll be there at six."

"I'll see you then," she replied, and hung up before he could say anything else.

Smiling for the first time in two days, he shoved back his chair and left his office to go find his brother.

Deborah didn't have to wait for Phoenix to arrive this time. He was on her doorstep when she drove up, pacing back and forth like an impatient panther. His truck was parked at the curb, so she pulled straight up her driveway and stopped, her gaze searching his as he walked toward her.

He was smiling, but it was different from the way he'd smiled at her before. The expression in his eyes was still darkly intent, but also affectionate as he opened her door for her. His step was lighter, as though a heavy weight had been lifted from his shoulders.

Stepping out, she gasped when she was pulled against him. His mouth covered hers in a brief but devastating kiss.

Raising his head, he said, "Hi."

"Hello."

He took her hand and drew her toward his Bronco. "Phoenix, what are you doing? I want to change my clothes."

His gaze raked over her coffee-colored slacks and pink safari-style shirt, cinched in at her waist with a leather belt. "You look okay."

She rolled her eyes as she hurried to keep up with him. "High praise indeed," she said dryly. She would liked to have washed off the smell of the hospital, but it was obvious she wasn't going to have that chance.

In a perfect world she would have been told where they were going, but she didn't expect perfection. She had reached the point where she would accept whatever it took in order to be with Phoenix. She'd been surprised when he'd called her at the hospital, and astonished when he'd asked her to spend the weekend with him. Now he was whisking her away as though they were late for a fire.

When he pulled into a curving driveway behind a truck she recognized, Phoenix didn't have to tell her where they were. They had parked behind that same truck the night they'd gone to the warehouse. The large ranch-style brick house belonged to his brother.

Denver met them at the door, an amused gleam in his eyes as he ushered them inside. His home was furnished in a southwestern style, with soft beiges, muted turquoise shades, and dashes of orange and sky blue. She noticed several pieces of Indian pottery in the living room and a beautiful woven blanket over the back of the couch. Unlike Phoenix, Denver openly surrounded himself with his Indian heritage.

Denver had crossed the room to the bar when his wife appeared in the doorway, He smiled at her. "I was about to offer our guests something to drink. Do we have time?"

"At least an hour," Courtney said, smiling as she stepped into the room. She hugged Phoenix and gave him a kiss on the cheek. "Hi, Phoenix."

Smiling down at her, Phoenix touched her nose with the tip of a finger, "Hi, Bo-peep."

Turning to Deborah, Courtney introduced herself. "I'm Courtney Sierra, and you must be Dr. Justin."

Courtney was wearing a skirt and blouse, both slightly rumpled, as though she'd worn the clothing all day. Deborah also noticed the brace on Courtney's left leg. She would like to ask her about her medical problems—Phoenix had told her Courtney had undergone surgery to correct a clubfoot—but this wasn't the time to indulge in professional curiosity.

"Deborah, please," she said as she shook Courtney's hand.

Courtney smiled. "All right. Deborah it is. How are you at major surgery? I have a couple of chickens that need cutting up, and I'm not very good at it."

"Do they have insurance?" Deborah asked, grinning.

"No, but we do if you cut a finger or two," Denver said. "Would you like something to drink before you go into surgery, Deborah?"

"No, thanks."

She followed Courtney into the kitchen, and the first thing she noticed was that dinner had a long way to go before it would be ready. Shopping bags were still sitting on a counter, and there was nothing cooking on the stove.

Considering Courtney apparently hadn't had time to change clothes, either, Deborah concluded this evening's dinner invitation had been a last-minute thing.

"Ah . . . Courtney, I'm probably out of line asking this, but were you expecting us?"

Courtney plunked two whole chickens onto a chopping board and handed her a large knife. "I could lie and say I'm just naturally unorganized, but I guess I wouldn't fool you, would I?"

"Well, you could try. You're right though, I probably wouldn't believe you. This was Phoenix's idea, wasn't it? Did you receive a phone call from him a little after three this afternoon?"

"From Denver," Courtney said, "saying Phoenix wanted to bring you over for dinner tonight. How did you know the time?"

"Because I got a phone call from Phoenix a few minutes before three." Deborah picked up the knife. "You've been around the Sierra men longer than I have, Courtney. Do you know what's going on?"

Courtney tilted her head to one side and looked at Deborah, an amused gleam in her brown eyes. "Did Phoenix tell you about Amethyst Rand, the country-western singer, being my mother?"

Puzzled about what one thing had to do with the other, she nodded and waited.

"My mother once had a hit song called, 'Courtin' Days and Honeymoon Nights.' I think that about sums it up. Part of courting is meeting the family. I think that's the purpose of this evening."

"I think you're reaching."

Courtney gave Deborah an assessing glance. "Phoenix has never brought a woman here before."

Deborah started carving one of the chickens. "I would like to think that means something, but I've discovered nothing is ever as it seems with Phoenix."

"Has he pulled a practical joke on you yet?"

"No, and it's worrying me. He said he only picks on people he likes. I'm only taking it a day at a time with Phoenix, not expecting too much."

"I'm not even going to dare give you any advice. I wouldn't have taken any when I started getting involved with Denver. But I will say I'm pleased to finally meet you. Denver told me about meeting you the night the teenagers broke into the warehouse, and I admit I was curious about you. You aren't the type of woman Phoenix has seen in the past. I hope everything works out for you two. He needs someone to care about him."

Pausing, Deborah looked at Courtney. "I don't know if he'll let me." Changing the subject, she asked, "Why does Phoenix call you Bo-peep?"

That question led to Courtney telling Deborah about the practical joke Phoenix had tried to pull on Denver. He'd put a goat in Denver's truck just before Denver had to pick up Courtney for a date. The joke had backfired on Phoenix when she and Denver took the goat to Phoenix's apartment. Ever since then, Phoenix had called her Bo-peep.

As the two women prepared the dinner, they used the opportunity to get acquainted. By the time the meal was on the table, they were firm friends.

Deborah still wasn't sure how things were working out between her and Phoenix several hours later when Phoenix drove her home. She'd enjoyed the dinner and the conversation, which had covered everything from Courtney's interest in history to her mother's and sisters' careers in country-western music, to a description of the plantation house

Sierra Construction had renovated for the famous singer. Interspersed were debates between Phoenix and Denver on the merits of various football teams. The evening had been comfortable and casual, and Deborah hoped it would be repeated.

As Phoenix turned the corner onto her street, she said, "I like your sister-in-law. She handled having unexpected dinner guests with a lot of style and grace."

Frowning, Phoenix pulled into her driveway behind her car. Sometimes it wasn't all that easy being involved with an intelligent woman. He should know by now not to underestimate her.

He turned off the engine and placed his arm on the back of the seat. "I wanted to be with you tonight, and I wanted you to meet Denver's wife, so I arranged to do both."

"Why did you want me to meet Courtney?"

"You've already met my brother. Courtney is the rest of my family."

"There's another member of your family. Your father."

He trailed the back of one finger down her cheek. "I see my father once a year. At Christmas. It usually lasts two hours, three hours tops. We tour the horse barns, make a few appropriate complimentary remarks, have a thimbleful of runny eggnog, then leave. I don't have the same relationship with my father you have with your parents."

She reached up to take his hand. "I still don't understand what the rush was for me to meet your sister-in-law."

He turned his hand over to grasp hers. "I've seen you with your family. I wanted you to see me with mine." Leaning over, he kissed her briefly. "Are you going to invite me in?"

It only took the touch of his mouth on hers to remind her of the magic she found in his arms. She might not understand what tomorrow would bring with Phoenix, but she did have tonight.

He kissed her again, and her lips parted under his as she sank into his desire. She met him as an equal, giving and receiving with matching hunger. He plundered, gripped, and whispered soft words. She invited, caressed, and trembled.

When she breathed his name, he lifted her over the consul and settled her across his thighs. "Do you know what you do to me?"

Her hands threaded through his hair as she brushed her lips over his jaw and the corners of his mouth. "I want to please you."

"Just being in the same room with you pleases me." His hand stroked her thigh, then slid between her legs. "We are so incredible together, and I don't want it to end. It won't end. We won't end."

Pushing open the door of the truck, he kept her securely against his chest and carried her to the town house. Using her key , he opened the door, then kicked it shut once they were inside. Lowering her to stand before him, he unclasped the buckle of her belt and let it drop to the floor. He kept her gaze locked with his as he unbuttoned her shirt and parted the front. His hands skimmed over her rib cage, her lacy bra, and her shoulders.

She shivered and swayed toward him, mesmerized by the heat in his eyes. He unclasped the front hook of her bra and swept it away. She closed her eyes when he lifted her and closed his mouth over the hardening tip of her breast. She cried out at the delicious sensations tightening her body and searing through her bloodstream.

Phoenix groaned when he heard the sound of her

arousal. The bedroom suddenly seemed too far away. He had to have her now, to be inside her now or go out of his mind. The fastening of her slacks opened under his fingers, and he tugged them down her slender hips.

"Put your arms around my neck," he ordered roughly after she'd stepped out of her clothing..

She obeyed.

"Open my jeans. I want your hands on me."

Again she obeyed, lowering the zipper with tantalizing slowness. She smiled when she heard his quick intake of breath as she took him in her hand.

"Deborah," he murmured.

He leaned back against the door and lifted her, wrapping her legs around his hips. "I have to be part of you. Now."

Her eyes started to close when she felt him push into her.

"No," he said. "Don't close your eyes. Look at me. I want to see your eyes when I come into you."

She met his avid gaze. He entered her deeply, hot and hard and relentless. Raising herself up, she tightened her hold around his neck and pressed against him.

"Tell me," he demanded, his voice raspy and urgent.

"What?" she asked, dazed by the sudden command.

"Say the words. I want to hear the words."

Distracted as she was, it took her a few seconds to realized what he wanted her to say.

"I love you, Phoenix Sky Sierra," she said softly. "I love you."

Some deep emotion flashed in his eyes, then he kissed her with tenderness mixed with desire.

He groaned with pleasure when she arched her

back and moved on him. He grasped her hips to control her movements, dazzled by the riot of sensations he found with her, the rich beauty of her response, which escalated his own to new heights. Her moist warmth enveloped him, surrounding him, and he willingly lost himself within her.

The soft explosion of completion caught them both. She cried out his name at the same time he whispered hers. Satisfaction rippled through them simultaneously, and their bodies convulsed with a shattering release.

Phoenix didn't ease his hold on her. He couldn't bear to be separated from her, even for the brief time it would take to go to her bedroom. His arms kept her locked to him as he carried her down the hall. In her bedroom he eased them down onto the bed and began the delicious sequence of passion all over again.

The sun was beginning to appear over the horizon when Phoenix sat down on the side of Deborah's bed, enjoying the freedom of being able to watch her as long as he wanted. Whatever he had done to deserve such a woman in his life, he could only be grateful he'd done it.

Just looking at her pleased him. He lifted a lock of hair away from her cheek, smiling when the silk strands curled around his finger. It reminded him of the way she had wrapped herself around his heart the first moment he'd seen her.

Trailing his finger down the side of her face, he smiled tenderly when she made a grumpy sound and turned her head. Touching her was a gift he would never take for granted.

He bent down and kissed her cheek. She stirred, and he kissed her again, this time on her lips.

She opened her eyes. It took her a few seconds to focus, then she smiled. "My dream came true."

"What dream is that?"

"To wake up and find you here."

He closed his teeth over her bottom lip, then kissed her. "I'd like to be with you again tonight. Is that all right with you?"

"I should be through at the hospital around seven." She turned to look at the bedside clock. "What time is it now?"

"You have an hour before you have to be at the hospital, according to the schedule I saw posted on your calendar in the kitchen. I was going to wake you up sooner, but I've been enjoying watching you sleep."

Her gaze lowered from his face to the shirt he was wearing. "You're leaving, aren't you?"

He nodded. "As much as I hate to go with you lying in bed all warm and naked, I need to get to work. I have some apologies to make, and I want to get it over with. And if I don't leave you now, we'll both be late for work."

"Apologies?" Holding the sheet to her chest, she sat up and leaned back against the headboard. "Did some of your practical jokes backfire again?"

"No chickens or goldfish this time. Just an exceptionally bad mood." He ran his fingers over the sheet, smoothing his hand across the shape of her. "I've rubbed a couple of people the wrong way the last few days."

She frowned and brushed her hand over her eyes as she tried to make sense out of what he was saying. "Why have you rubbed people the wrong way?"

He smiled. Her hair was tousled and snarled, her

eyes sleepy and only partially opened. "You have to be the most gorgeous woman in the world," he murmured as he leaned forward to kiss her.

He lingered over her lips, taking his time, and Deborah didn't mind one bit. When he raised his head, she murmured, "It's hard to imagine you humble and apologizing all over the place. What caused your bad mood?"

"I was just a little cranky until I came to my senses. I finally figured out what was important and what wasn't. Now I need to apologize to Belle and one of our supervisors."

She touched the side of his face. "What did you decide is important?" she asked, taking a chance that he would give her the answer she wanted to hear.

"Having you in my life." He sat up, putting necessary distance between them. "You'd better get moving, Doc, or you'll be late. The coffee will be ready by the time you get out of the shower. I wish I could join you, but I have to get going. Give me one more kiss."

He made it a long kiss. It was going to have to last him all day.

During the next couple of days, Deborah felt as though she were on a merry-go-round, with work occupying the better part of her days and Phoenix taking up her nights. Her life had suddenly become very full and required some serious juggling of her time in order to fit everything in. If she was getting less sleep, it was an easy sacrifice to make, for that was when she was in Phoenix's arms.

She didn't want off the merry-go-round, either, not as long as it meant she would be with Phoenix. She wanted to grab the brass ring. She wanted forever.

Phoenix seemed to have different priorities. After dinner Thursday night he took her to the Sierra Construction complex and introduced her to several large pieces of equipment, various construction supplies, and his office. She found everything interesting and informative. And confusing. It wasn't that she didn't enjoy seeing such an important part of his life. She did. She just couldn't understand why he was going to such lengths to show her every nook and cranny of his business.

She would have asked him, but as soon as they arrived back at her town house, he swept her up in his arms and carried her into her bedroom.

He was waiting for her when she arrived home on Friday. She had called in the favor from Rob for filling in for him the night his baby was born, and had arranged for him to take her place at the free clinic on Saturday. Early that morning she'd packed enough casual clothes for two days, per Phoenix's instructions. When she'd asked the reasonable question about where they were going, he only said there was a place he wanted her to see and they wouldn't be back until Sunday.

The place turned out to be a log cabin in a peaceful valley near Charlottesville, Virginia, about a two-hour drive away. Nestled in among tall fir trees, the cabin sat near a small lake. The only sign of other inhabitants were the sounds of birds and the flutter of wings when they were disturbed.

Compared to his opulent apartment, the cabin could best be called rustic. Its one room boasted a wood-frame couch and a chair and a stone fireplace that took up the better part of one wall. A small table was tucked against another wall, with two wooden chairs pulled up to it. In the center of the table was a kerosene lamp. A large trunk sat on the floor behind the couch.

Deborah looked for but couldn't see any evidence of his woodworking. As private as Phoenix was, this would seem the perfect place for him to do his carving, yet apparently he didn't.

There was a bed up in an open loft, which could be reached by wooden steps built into the wall opposite the fireplace. It was obvious cooking was not one of the priorities, considering the kitchen consisted of a two-burner camp stove. There was running water, as long as someone "ran" to the well behind the cabin to bring it inside. The other important item of civilized living consisted of a small building at some distance from the cabin and the well. There was a small half-moon carved into the door.

Deborah laughed merrily when she spotted the outhouse, and Phoenix looked taken aback. "I thought you'd be horrified and want to go screaming back to civilization. I didn't expect you to laugh about the primitive plumbing."

"Is that what your other guests have done?"

He shook his head. "I've never brought anyone here before except Denver. He helped me build it. I wouldn't mind Courtney being here, but it would be difficult for her to manage the rough terrain." He gave her an odd look when he saw she was still smiling. "What do you find so funny about an out-house?"

"It made me think of some of the less than pristine facilities from my childhood, especially the one made of a length of canvas stretched across four poles that were stuck into the ground. To get in, the adults had to pull one of the poles out of the dirt, then replace it once they were inside. There was just enough room for one person. We kids found it much more fun to crawl under the canvas since it hung about a foot off the ground. I don't know how old I was at the time, but I remember just being able to look over the top of the canvas when I stood up inside. This." —she gestured toward the outhouse—"is like a palace compared to that."

He touched her cheek to turn her face toward him. "I keep underestimating you."

She reciprocated by stroking his cheek, too, enjoying the feel of his rougher skin. "And you keep surprising me. I probably should have expected you to have something like this remote cabin. You're a very private person, Phoenix. You don't let many people get close to you. I'm glad you're finally letting me in."

His arms came around her, and he held her against him. "As I said, I keep underestimating you. I thought I was taking a big chance in bringing you here. You might have thought I was nuts for having a cabin so far away from civilization."

Raising her head from his chest, she looked at the solidly built cabin. He was beginning to trust her, even though he still had reservations.

"I can see why you wouldn't want too many people to see this place. It doesn't really fit your image."

He stiffened, then loosened his hold so he could see her face. "What image?"

"The practical joker, the apartment straight out of the red-light district, and the kiss-off roses sent to scores of women after taking them out only a couple of times. Those are all props, like a clown's makeup hiding the deeper feelings of the man underneath."

He looked as if he'd just been run over by one of those heavy-duty pieces of equipment at Sierra Construction.

She smiled. "You need this remote place like your

mother needed books. We all need something or someplace where we can recharge our batteries and be ourselves."

"What about you? Do you have such a place?"

"When I was young, I used to climb trees and go as high as I could where I'd be hidden by the leaves. I'd stay there and dream about all sorts of things I was going to do when I was older. Finding a private place in a carnival isn't all that easy to do, so I would hunt for a tree wherever we were."

"And now?"

"I thought having a place of my own that wasn't on wheels would be it, but it isn't."

"There are plenty of trees here," he said, his gaze intent on her face.

"You want me to come here again?"

He brushed a kiss over her lips. "Yes. In fact, I might even insist on it."

She knew he wasn't making the offer lightly. "I just might take you up on that."

He grinned. "Good." Sweeping her up in his arms, he started walking toward the cabin. "I have something else I want to share with you, and this can't wait."

Later that evening as they were sitting in front of a gently burning fire, Deborah held his hand in hers and ran her thumb over his scarred fingertips.

"When are you going to tell me about your wood carving, Phoenix?"

She'd expected him to tense up at her question, but he didn't. Instead he smiled and lifted her hand to his mouth. "Your curiosity again, Doc?"

"I've seen the Indian village in your spare room. You can yell at me for snooping, and you would be right, but I don't regret seeing it. Your work is beautiful, and you should be very proud of it, not hide it away where no one can see it."

"I don't do it for anyone but myself." He touched his tongue to first one finger, then the next, until he'd moistened each finger. "It's not easy for me to open myself up for another person's inspection, Deborah. You're going to have to be patient with me. I am trying."

"Is that why I had the tour of the construction company and went to your brother's house for dinner? So that I could see other parts of your life?"

"Something like that."

He moved away from her and went over to the trunk. The clasps were well oiled and opened easily. Propping the lid open, he gestured for her to come closer.

Peering inside, Deborah saw carving tools laid out on a tray and small blocks of wood in various stages of completion. She ran her finger over a fox partially emerging from a hollow log. The detail was incredible, and she marveled at his talent.

"When I saw the carving you'd done on the Indian village, I knew the man behind the practical joker had more depth and deeper feelings than anyone I'd ever met." She looked up at him. "Thank you for showing me your work, Phoenix. You won't regret sharing it with me."

Combing his fingers through her hair, he held her in place as he lowered his head. "The only thing I'll regret is if I ever hurt you."

"Just don't regret sharing yourself with me, Phoenix. You can trust me. I love you."

He ran his tongue along her bottom lip. "I never thought I wanted a woman to say that to me. Now I can't hear it enough."

She closed her eyes as he lowered her onto the rug in front of the fire. Before she became immersed in sensual sensations, she wished he could have said the same words to her. Then he filled his mouth with her breasts, and she couldn't think of anything but him.

Ten

When they returned to Richmond late Sunday afternoon, Phoenix made the turn that would take them to his apartment. As usual, Deborah grumbled silently, because he hadn't asked her first where she wanted to go. Up until now she hadn't complained because it hadn't mattered, but this time she protested.

"Phoenix, I'd rather go to my place."

He hesitated for a few seconds, then changed directions and drove toward her town house. "I guess I can wait."

"Wait for what?" she asked, puzzled by his resigned tone of voice.

"There was something I wanted to show you in my apartment, but I'll save it for another time."

Since she'd seen all of his apartment except for the spare room, she wondered if he had planned to show her his wood carving. He had told her about it, though, and for now that was enough. They had come a long way toward a closer relationship the last couple of days, and she was greedy enough to want to go the distance toward complete trust. But that was still far away. He had yet to tell her he loved her. Not once during the long passion-filled nights at the cabin had he admitted his feelings for her, other than desire.

He also hadn't said anything about a future with her. She wanted to think he was opening up to her by showing her the important parts of his life, like Sierra Construction and the cabin. Being a realist, though, she had to remind herself she might be suffering from a severe case of wishful thinking, wanting a future with this wary man.

When Phoenix pulled into Deborah's car driveway, they saw Stan's car parked in front of Belle's house. Before Phoenix could open his door, Stan burst out of Belle's town house and marched toward them.

"Uh-oh," Deborah said. "I think your presence is being requested."

She stayed in the Bronco as Phoenix met Stan halfway between the two town houses. She could see by the serious expression on Stan's face that there was a problem. As she watched, Phoenix nodded, then walked back to her. He opened her door. "Deborah?" he said hesitantly.

"I know." She jumped down out of the Bronco. "You need to go with Stan to help one of your kids."

"You're good, Doc." He grabbed her overnight bag and walked her to her front door. "You're not only beautiful, you read minds."

"It wasn't all that difficult to figure out." She dug out her house key and slipped it into the lock. "Are some kids in trouble?"

"Stan's partner has a nephew who's gotten in with a bad crowd. Stan wants to try to talk to him before he does something stupid. I know some of the kids he's been hanging around with, so Stan wants me along."

"You'd better get going then." She looked back over her shoulder and saw Stan was watching them, waiting for Phoenix. "It's important."

"So are you." He sighed heavily. "I really hate to leave you like this. I had other plans for this evening."

She touched his face. "There will be other evenings." She hoped. When he hesitated, she added, "It's all right, Phoenix. I understand why you have to go with Stan. I don't expect you to stop working with the kids because you're seeing me."

"Seeing you," he murmured. "That's a pretty tame way to describe our relationship."

She was open to suggestions. What would he call their relationship? she wondered. But she wasn't sure she was ready to hear his answer.

"We'll discuss it later." He leaned down to kiss her. "I'll call you tonight if it isn't too late."

She shook her head. "You're going to be busy enough tonight. I'll talk to you tomorrow."

Torn, he kissed her again, longer and harder. Finally, he raised his head. "I don't like it, but I suppose you're right. I'll have to settle for tomorrow."

She nodded and went inside. For a few minutes she simply leaned against her door. Helping troubled teenagers was as much a part of Phoenix as the wood carving, the rustic cabin, and his construction company. She wasn't just being polite when she'd told him she understood why he had to leave.

She could only hope that his having a commitment to troubled teens meant it was possible Phoenix would be able to make a commitment to her.

As she thought about all they'd shared, she smiled when she realized one of the things bothering her was that he had never pulled one of his infamous practical jokes on her. Knowing him as she did, she understood that he chose Belle and Denver to be the recipients of his practical jokes because he trusted them to still care for him no matter what he did.

It was one test she had left to take, and maybe a silly test by some people's standards. But it would be proof that he trusted her enough to know she would love him regardless of what irritating prank he pulled on her.

But she couldn't pass the test if it was never offered to her.

Considering all the other things they needed to work out, the lack of practical jokes seemed a strange thing for her to be dwelling on. Still, she couldn't help wondering if he would ever include her in the small circle of people he trusted.

Fate had brought them together originally. Now fate seemed destined to keep them apart.

The flu virus that had descended on the Richmond area two weeks earlier hit the hospital staff without any remorse, claiming victims from the chief of staff to the janitor. Deborah had to do the work of four people, with doctors, lab technicians, radiologists, and nurses calling in sick. Since the flu epidemic wasn't exclusive to the hospital, the waiting room was overflowing with patients too.

Deborah barely had time to eat or sleep, much less spend even a spare moment with Phoenix. He wasn't too happy when she called him two days in a row to tell him she wouldn't be able to see him that night and didn't have a clue when she would be free. He understood her situation since he had been called upon to fill in for some of his workmen who had been laid low with the flu. That didn't mean he liked it.

By Thursday he was less understanding than he had been earlier in the week. It wasn't only that he missed their lovemaking. He missed her. During the previous week he'd got used to have her next to him at night. Now he found it impossible to sleep without her in bed with him. He was also concerned because she was working so hard. Her days were even longer than his, and he didn't like the fact that she was exposed to every germ and virus going around.

One of the revelations about being in love he had to accept was worrying about Deborah more than himself.

A little after five on Thursday he was just getting into his Bronco when his brother pulled up alongside him. He walked over the the truck as Denver rolled down his window.

"Are you calling it a day?" Denver asked.

"I might as well. I don't seem to be accomplishing much with the small work force we have left. How about you?"

"I'm going home. Courtney looked a little pale this morning. I hope she isn't coming down with this flu, especially since she thinks she might be expecting a little Sierra."

Phoenix grinned at Denver and leaned his arms on the window frame. "How do you feel about becoming a daddy, big brother?"

"Stunned, excited, scared, thrilled. You name it. I've run the gamut of emotions since she told me she might be pregnant." He smiled. "I imagine they're about the same emotions you're going through with Deborah. You want her more than anything else in this world, but marriage is a daunting prospect.

When are you gong to stop fighting the inevitable and marry the woman?"

Frowning, Phoenix pushed himself away from the truck. "Right now, I'd just like to be able to see her for more than five minutes at a stretch. If this epidemic goes on much longer, she's going to forget what I look like."

Denver chuckled. "You'll just have to remind her then, won't you? I'll see you tomorrow."

Phoenix lifted his hand in a wave as Denver put his truck in gear and drove away. Getting into his Bronco, he sat still for a moment, not starting the engine. The last thing he wanted to do was go back to his empty apartment. He wanted to see Deborah.

Denver had a point. It was time for Phoenix to remind Deborah what he looked like.

Without bothering to change clothes, he drove to the hospital and walked straight into the emergency room. Ignoring the admissions clerks and the triage nurse, he pushed opened the swinging doors leading to the treatment rooms and walked up to the nurses' station.

The nurse on duty looked at him curiously. "Can I help you?"

"I'm looking for Dr. Justin."

"She's with a patient right now." Her professional gaze swept briskly over him, from the top of his head to his work boots. Her expression made it clear that didn't think he was in much need of medical attention. "If you'll go to the waiting room, we'll call you as soon as we can, Mr. . . . ?"

"Sierra. I'm not here as a patient. Where can I wait for Deborah?"

Obviously baffled by the request, the nurse glanced around, as though looking for just such a place and coming up empty. "Perhaps the cafeteria?"

Just then Deborah came out of a cubicle and saw Phoenix. Surprise, curiosity, but most of all pleasure, flickered in her eyes. The pleasure remained as she walked toward him.

She handed a medical record to the nurse. "I'm releasing Mrs. Barrenson, Sally. Would you go over the medication with her, please? The prescriptions are in the file."

"Sure." Sally looked from Deborah to Phoenix, grinned, then left. There would be something to talk about in the nurse's lounge that evening other than the number of patients they'd treated.

Phoenix took Deborah's hand and drew her away from the nurses' station. He stroked the shadows under her eyes with one finger. "Dammit, Deborah. You're going to make yourself sick if you don't get some rest."

She was touched by his concern, and had to resist the desire to lean against him. "It's nothing twenty-four hours of sleep won't cure." She raised her hand to his lips before he could object again. "I am tired, but so is everyone else who's doing double shifts. It can't be helped. I'm used to this, Phoenix. I'll be fine."

He was aware of the curious glances they were receiving from the staff, and even a few patients. He decided to give them something to think about other than the flu.

Lowering his head, he kissed Deborah. She stiffened for an instant, then her eyes closed, and she sank into him with the natural response he was becoming addicted to and didn't want to live without.

After a long kiss he reluctantly released her. Her lips were moist, her tired eyes slightly dazed with arousal. If he had his choice, he would pick her up, carry her away from the hospital, and make love to her until the sun came up. Maybe longer.

It was proof of how in love she was that Deborah wasn't angry at him. She just shook her head in mock exasperation. "What am I going to do with you, Mr. Sierra? You're disrupting the smooth running of this emergency room."

He didn't smile as she'd expected. "I'm worried about you, dammit. You're working too hard."

"Belle told me you and Denver are having to take on more work because of sick employees too. This epidemic has hit everyone. It's finally easing up, though, so it shouldn't be too much longer before things are back to normal."

"I hope so." He shoved his hands into his pockets to fight the temptation to pull her back into his arms. "After we're married, we're going to have to come to some sort of compromise about our work so we can have enough time together. Not seeing you is killing me."

"Married?"

Heads turned, eyes widened, and grins broadened, when Deborah shouted a word that had nothing to do with the flu, medicine, or hospital business.

Lowering her voice, she asked, "Who said we were getting married?"

"I think I just did. Why do you look so surprised? You said you loved me. Don't you want to get married?"

Crossing her arms, she glared at him. "I would give it some serious thought if I was ever asked, but I don't recall being asked. You've never even said you loved me."

Irritated, he raised his voice. "If I didn't love you, why would I be asking you to marry me?"

"You love me?"

"Hell, yes, I love you." He was practically shouting.

The smattering of applause startled them both, reminding them of where they were.

Deborah groaned aloud. Damn the man. He had to have the world's worst timing.

She took a step back from him and adjusted the collar of her white coat. It was a little late to try to recover her professional demeanor, but she gave it a noble attempt.

"We'll discuss this later," she said under her breath.

"Among other things." Unabashed by the growing audience, he asked, "How late do you have to work?"

She shook her head wearily. "I don't know. Maybe only until eleven if Bill Freeden is feeling better and can come in."

"I don't care what time it is, I have to see you. I'll be here at eleven to drive you home."

"I can't guarantee I'll be able to leave then. You might end up having to wait around for hours."

"Come to my place whenever you get off then. I'm not going to go another night without you."

A nurse approached her with a medical record in her hand. "I'm sorry, Dr. Justin, but the patient the rescue squad just brought in needs to be seen right away."

"I'll be right there, Janey. I have to go, Phoenix."

"I know." He touched her cheek. "I'll be waiting."

For a moment she thought he was going to kiss her again, then was devastated when he didn't. He only stroked her face and then turned and left.

During the next several hours Deborah fielded questions about her marriage plans and accepted words of congratulations, as word of her scene with Phoenix filtered from the emergency room to the rest of the hospital. She was thankful she was kept busy with patients, so she didn't have to try to come up with answers that didn't make her sound incredibly stupid. Like when was she getting married? She hadn't the faintest idea. She couldn't very well admit that tonight was the first night she'd heard Phoenix planned on marrying her.

Nor could she admit how her heart was still pounding as though she'd dashed up ten flights of stairs without stopping. Phoenix had actually said he wanted to marry her! Unbelievable.

As the night wore on, she became more impatient to see Phoenix, to talk to him, to hear him say he loved her. Over and over again. Maybe then she would be able to believe it.

It was almost midnight before she was finally able to leave the hospital. Bill had dragged himself into the emergency room after being declared fit enough for duty. He looked like he would have benefited from at least another day of rest, but he gamely put his stethoscope around his neck and reached for a medical record.

The cool night air was bracing and did a great deal to wake Deborah up at she walked out to her car with Sally. The nurse was dying for details about the romance going on in Dr. Justin's life.

"To think it all started when he came into the emergency room," Sally said. "I keep telling my mother that I meet a lot of men at work, but she doesn't believe me. Wait until I tell her about your fiancé."

Her fiancé, Deborah thought with awe. She tried to make the appropriate comments, but decided there really weren't any. She was as astounded as Sally and the rest of the staff by the proposal she'd received in the midst of patients and co-workers.

It might not have been moonlight and roses, but

she certainly wouldn't ever forget the night Phoenix stated they were getting married.

They reached Sally's car first, and she said good night before walking on to her car. When she reached it, she saw a piece of white paper was stuck under the windshield wiper on the driver's side. She got into the car, turned on the overhead light, and read: *Drive carefully. The life you save is mine.*

It wasn't signed, not even with the drawing of a phoenix rising up from flames. She folded it carefully and tucked it into her pocket.

At his apartment building the space next to his Bronco was vacant, and she pulled into it. She had taken him at his word that he would be waiting for her, no matter what time she arrived.

She licked her lips nervously as she punched the elevator button for the fourth floor. Her stomach felt as though it had been left behind when the elevator started to rise. A fine sheen of perspiration coated her skin, and her breathing was erratic. She giggled at the automatic thought that came to mind. She should see a doctor.

But she didn't have the flu. She was nervous. She was petrified. She felt like an idiot for being either one. What did she expect him to do when she arrived? she asked herself. Did she think he was going to say he hadn't really meant it?

On shaky legs she stepped out of the elevator and walked down the hall to Phoenix's apartment. She lifted her hand to knock, but before she could, the door opened, and Phoenix was drawing her inside.

"I was about ready to come after you," he said just before his mouth settled on hers with naked possession.

His kiss helped dispel some of her nervousness, replacing it with a tension of a different kind.

He slowly released her and moved back. She took two steps into the living room, then stopped cold.

"Ah, Phoenix. Have you noticed you've been robbed?"

He let his gaze roam over his living room, his empty living room. Empty except for the painting of the Indian maiden, which was still hanging on the wall. All that remained of the furniture were imprints in the carpet.

He took her hand and led her into the room. "The Salvation Army has the furniture except for the entertainment center. I put that in storage."

"Why?"

"Because I occasionally listen to music and watch a little television."

She gave him a pained expression. "Not why did you put the entertainment center in storage. Why did you get rid of all your furniture?"

"It won't fit in the new house."

Maybe she'd got off on the wrong floor, she thought. Or maybe she'd fallen asleep and was just having a strange dream. "New house? What new house?"

"Our new house. The one Sierra Construction is going to build just as soon as we pick out the land and choose the house plans."

Her legs felt like rubber, yet her mind couldn't seem to stretch to absorb everything he was saying. She held up her hand to slow him down.

"What happened to the man who didn't plan on getting married?"

"He fell in love."

"When?"

"I think the first night I met you in the emergency room. It just took me a while to realize it."

She drew in a deep breath, but it didn't help. She

was still feeling dizzy, as though she'd been spun around too many times.

"You sure are making up for lost time," she said dryly.

He wrapped his arms around her and held her securely against him. "I didn't plan on telling you at the hospital tonight. I was going to take you to a romantic restaurant after we got back from the cabin last Sunday, then bring you back here where I could show you that I'd gotten rid of the furniture. But Stan got in the way, then the flu epidemic came up, and I've hardly seen you. Tonight I couldn't wait any longer."

"I noticed. So did everyone in the emergency room."

There was no apology in his gaze or on his lips when he smiled down at her. "So when will you marry me?"

She stepped away from him. "I can't believe I'm saying this, but I don't think we should get married."

He stalked after her and swept her up into his arms. When he carried her into his bedroom, she saw that the Salvation Army hadn't taken his bed.

"What are you doing?" she asked when he put her down. "I tell you I don't think we should get married, and you carry me off to bed?"

"You're obviously exhausted and aren't thinking straight. After a good night's sleep, you'll be able to give me the right answer in the morning."

Sitting up, she held out her hand. "Sit down, Phoenix."

He took her hand and sat. "Explain."

"I thought I wanted you to ask me to marry you more than I wanted anything in my life, but it wouldn't work."

"Why not?"

"I believe you when you say you love me, but I don't think you trust me."

"Trust you? Of course I trust you. I love you."

"They aren't the same thing."

"Why don't you think I trust you? I've told you more about myself than I've ever told anyone. I've shown you parts of my life I've never shown anyone else before. What would you call that if it isn't trust?"

"Then why haven't you annoyed me with any practical jokes?"

He blinked. "What?"

"You said you only pull practical jokes on people you like. Does that mean you love me but you don't like me?"

He got up off the bed and took several steps away. Throwing his hands in the air, he muttered, "I don't believe this. I'm in love with a crazy woman."

"I know it sounds strange, but I can't help but worry that you aren't being yourself with me. We won't last very long if you're always on your best behavior and not being your real self."

"Like I said. You're crazy." He shoved his hand into the front pocket of his jeans and pulled out a small velvet box. Returning to the bed, he sat down and picked up her hand. Holding it palm up, he set the box in it. "Open it."

"Haven't you listened to anything I've said? I don't think we should get married."

"I heard you. Open the box anyway."

"Phoenix."

"Deborah, open the box."

"I'm not going to put on your ring, Phoenix. Not until we talk this out."

"Tell me that after you've looked at the ring—then I'll back off."

Since she couldn't think of a reason to refuse, she opened the box.

A dozen tiny silk butterflies flew out of the box and fluttered onto the bed and her lap. She picked one up and stared at it, then she threw herself into his arms.

"You do love me."

He shook his head as he swept the butterflies off the bed and took the ring out of the box. He pressed her down onto the mattress. "That's what I've been trying to tell you. Are you going to put the ring on?"

"You put it on."

After he slid the ring on her finger, he kissed her hand, then her mouth.

"*Now* will you marry me?"

"Yes."

"And live happily ever after?"

"I guarantee it."

THE EDITOR'S CORNER

There's a lot to look forward to from LOVESWEPT in October—five fabulous stories from your favorites, and a delightful novel from an exciting new author. You know you can always rely on LOVESWEPT to provide six top-notch—and thrilling—romances each and every month.

Leading the lineup is Marcia Evanick, with **SWEET TEMPTATION,** LOVESWEPT #570. And sweet temptation is just what Augusta Bodine is, as Garrison Fisher soon finds out. Paleontologist Garrison thinks the Georgia peach can't survive roughing it in his dusty dinosaur-fossil dig—but she meets his skepticism with bewitching stubbornness and a wildfire taste for adventure that he quickly longs to explore . . . and satisfy. Marcia is at her best with this heartwarming and funny romance.

Strange occurrences and the magic of love are waiting for you on board the **SCARLET BUTTERFLY,** LOVESWEPT #571, by Sandra Chastain. Ever since Sean Rogan restored the ancient—and possibly haunted—ship, he'd been prepared for anything, except the woman he finds sleeping in his bunk! The rogue sea captain warns Carolina Evans that he's no safe haven in a storm, but she's intent on fulfilling a promise made long ago, a promise of love. Boldly imaginative, richly emotional, **SCARLET BUTTERFLY** is a winner from Sandra.

Please give a big welcome to new author Leanne Banks and her very first LOVESWEPT, **GUARDIAN ANGEL,** #572. In this enchanting romance Talia McKenzie is caught in the impossible situation of working very closely with Trace Barringer on a charity drive. He'd starred in her teenage daydreams, but now there's bad blood between their families. What is she to do, especially when Trace wants nothing less from her than her love? The answer makes for one surefire treat. Enjoy one of our New Faces of 1992!

Ever-popular Fayrene Preston creates a blazing inferno of desire in **IN THE HEAT OF THE NIGHT,** LOVESWEPT #573. Philip Killane expects trouble when Jacey finally comes home after so many years, for he's never forgotten the night she'd branded him with her fire, the night that had nearly ruined their lives. But he isn't prepared for the fact that his stepsister is more gorgeous than ever . . . or that he wants a second chance. An utterly sensational romance, with passion at its most potent—only from Fayrene!

In Gail Douglas's new LOVESWEPT, **THE LADY IS A SCAMP,** #574, the lady in the title is event planner Victoria Chase. She's usually poised and elegant, but businessman Dan Stewart upsets her equilibrium. Maybe it's his handshake that sets her on fire, or the intense blue eyes that see right inside her soul. She should be running to the hills instead of straight into his arms. This story showcases the winning charm of Gail's writing—plus a puppet and a clown who show our hero and heroine the path to love.

We end the month with **FORBIDDEN DREAMS** by Judy Gill, LOVESWEPT #575. When Jason O'Keefe blows back into Shell Landry's life with all the force of the winter storm howling outside her isolated cabin, they become trapped together in a cocoon of pleasure. Jason needs her to expose a con artist, and he also needs her kisses. Shell wants to trust him, but so much is at stake, including the secret that had finally brought her peace. Judy will leave you breathless with the elemental force raging between these two people.

On sale this month from FANFARE are three exciting novels. In **DAWN ON A JADE SEA** Jessica Bryan, the award-winning author of **ACROSS A WINE-DARK SEA,** once more intertwines romance, fantasy, and ancient history to create an utterly spellbinding story. Set against the stunning pageantry of ancient China, **DAWN ON A JADE SEA** brings together Rhea, a merperson from an undersea world, and Red Tiger, a son of merchants who has vowed revenge against the powerful nobleman who destroyed his family.

Now's your chance to grab a copy of **BLAZE,** by bestselling author Susan Johnson, and read the novel that won the *Romantic Times* award for Best Sensual Historical Romance and a Golden Certificate from *Affaire de Coeur* "for the quality, excellence of writing, entertainment and enjoyment it gave the readers." In this sizzling novel a Boston heiress is swept into a storm of passion she's never imagined, held spellbound by an Absarokee Indian who knows every woman's desires. . . .

Anytime we publish a book by Iris Johansen, it's an event—and **LAST BRIDGE HOME** shows why. Original, emotional, and sensual, it's romantic suspense at its most compelling. It begins with Jon Sandell, a man with many secrets and one remarkable power, appearing at Elizabeth Ramsey's cottage. When he reveals that he's there to protect her from danger, Elizabeth doesn't know whether this mesmerizing stranger is friend or foe. . . .

Also on sale this month in the Doubleday hardcover edition is **LADY DEFIANT** by Suzanne Robinson, a thrilling historical romance that brings back Blade, who was introduced in **LADY GALLANT.** Now Blade is one of Queen Elizabeth's most dangerous spies, and he must romance a beauty named Oriel who holds a clue that could alter the course of history.

Happy reading!

With warmest wishes,

Nita Taublib

Nita Taublib
Associate Publisher
LOVESWEPT and FANFARE

OFFICIAL RULES TO WINNERS CLASSIC SWEEPSTAKES

No Purchase necessary. To enter the sweepstakes follow instructions found elsewhere in this offer. You can also enter the sweepstakes by hand printing your name, address, city, state and zip code on a 3" x 5" piece of paper and mailing it to: Winners Classic Sweepstakes, P.O. Box 785, Gibbstown, NJ 08027. Mail each entry separately. Sweepstakes begins 12/1/91. Entries must be received by 6/1/93. Some presentations of this sweepstakes may feature a deadline for the Early Bird prize. If the offer you receive does, then to be eligible for the Early Bird prize your entry must be received according to the Early Bird date specified. Not responsible for lost, late, damaged, misdirected, illegible or postage due mail. Mechanically reproduced entries are not eligible. All entries become property of the sponsor and will not be returned.

Prize Selection/Validations: Winners will be selected in random drawings on or about 7/30/93, by VENTURA ASSOCIATES, INC., an independent judging organization whose decisions are final. Odds of winning are determined by total number of entries received. Circulation of this sweepstakes is estimated not to exceed 200 million. Entrants need not be present to win. All prizes are guaranteed to be awarded and delivered to winners. Winners will be notified by mail and may be required to complete an affidavit of eligibility and release of liability which must be returned within 14 days of date of notification or alternate winners will be selected. Any guest of a trip winner will also be required to execute a release of liability. Any prize notification letter or any prize returned to a participating sponsor, Bantam Doubleday Dell Publishing Group, Inc., its participating divisions or subsidiaries, or VENTURA ASSOCIATES, INC. as undeliverable will be awarded to an alternate winner. Prizes are not transferable. No multiple prize winners except as may be necessary due to unavailability, in which case a prize of equal or greater value will be awarded. Prizes will be awarded approximately 90 days after the drawing. All taxes, automobile license and registration fees, if applicable, are the sole responsibility of the winners. Entry constitutes permission (except where prohibited) to use winners' names and likenesses for publicity purposes without further or other compensation.

Participation: This sweepstakes is open to residents of the United States and Canada, except for the province of Quebec. This sweepstakes is sponsored by Bantam Doubleday Dell Publishing Group, Inc. (BDD), 666 Fifth Avenue, New York, NY 10103. Versions of this sweepstakes with different graphics will be offered in conjunction with various solicitations or promotions by different subsidiaries and divisions of BDD. Employees and their families of BDD, its division, subsidiaries, advertising agencies, and VENTURA ASSOCIATES, INC., are not eligible.

Canadian residents, in order to win, must first correctly answer a time limited arithmetical skill testing question. Void in Quebec and wherever prohibited or restricted by law. Subject to all federal, state, local and provincial laws and regulations.

Prizes: The following values for prizes are determined by the manufacturers' suggested retail prices or by what these items are currently known to be selling for at the time this offer was published. Approximate retail values include handling and delivery of prizes. Estimated maximum retail value of prizes: 1 Grand Prize ($27,500 if merchandise or $25,000 Cash); 1 First Prize ($3,000); 5 Second Prizes ($400 each); 35 Third Prizes ($100 each); 1,000 Fourth Prizes ($9.00 each) ; 1 Early Bird Prize ($5,000); Total approximate maximum retail value is $50,000. Winners will have the option of selecting any prize offered at level won. Automobile winner must have a valid driver's license at the time the car is awarded. Trips are subject to space and departure availability. Certain black-out dates may apply. Travel must be completed within one year from the time the prize is awarded. Minors must be accompanied by an adult. Prizes won by minors will be awarded in the name of parent or legal guardian.

For a list of Major Prize Winners (available after 7/30/93): send a self-addressed, stamped envelope entirely separate from your entry to: Winners Classic Sweepstakes Winners, P.O. Box 825, Gibbstown, NJ 08027. Requests must be received by 6/1/93. DO NOT SEND ANY OTHER CORRESPONDENCE TO THIS P.O. BOX.

The Delaney Dynasty lives on in

𝕿𝖍𝖊 𝕯𝖊𝖑𝖆𝖓𝖊𝖞 𝕮𝖍𝖗𝖎𝖘𝖙𝖒𝖆𝖘 𝕮𝖆𝖗𝖔𝖑

by Kay Hooper, Iris Johansen, & Fayrene Preston

Three of romantic fiction's best-loved authors present the changing face of Christmas spirit—past, present, and future—as they tell the story of three generations of Delaneys in love.

CHRISTMAS PAST by Iris Johansen

From the moment he first laid eyes on her, Kevin Delaney felt a curious attraction for the ragclad Gypsy beauty rummaging through the attic of his ranch at Killara. He didn't believe for a moment her talk of magic mirrors and second-sight, but something about Zara St. Cloud stirred his blood. Now, as Christmas draws near, a touch leads to a kiss and a gift of burning passion.

CHRISTMAS PRESENT by Fayrene Preston

Bria Delaney had been looking for Christmas ornaments in her mother's attic, when she saw him in the mirror for the first time—a stunningly handsome man with sky-blue eyes and red-gold hair. She had almost convinced herself he was only a dream when Kells Braxton arrived at Killara and led them both to a holiday wonderland of sensuous pleasure.

CHRISTMAS FUTURE by Kay Hooper

As the last of the Delaney men, Brett returned to Killara this Christmastime only to find it in the capable hands of his father's young and beautiful widow. Yet the closer he got to Cassie, the more Brett realized that the embers of their old love still burned and that all it would take was a look, a kiss, a caress, to turn their dormant passion into an inferno.

The best in Women's Fiction from Bantam FANFARE.
On sale in November 1992 AN 428 8/92

FANFARE

On Sale in August

DAWN ON A JADE SEA

☐ 29837-2 $5.50/6.50 in Canada
by Jessica Bryan

bestselling author of ACROSS A WINE-DARK SEA

She was a shimmering beauty from a kingdom of legend. A vision had brought Rhea to the glorious city of Ch'ang-an, compelling her to seek a green-eyed, auburn-haired foreign warrior called Zhao, the Red Tiger. Amid the jasmine of the Imperial Garden, passion will be born, hot as fire, strong as steel, eternal as the ocean tides.

BLAZE

☐ 29957-3 $5.50/6.50 in Canada
by Susan Johnson

bestselling author of FORBIDDEN and SINFUL

To Blaze Braddock, beautiful, pampered daughter of a millionaire, the American gold rush was a chance to flee the stifling codes of Boston society. But when Jon Hazard Black, a proud young Absarokee chief, challenged her father's land claim, Blaze was swept up in a storm of passions she had never before even imagined.

LAST BRIDGE HOME

☐ 29871-2 $4.50/5.50 in Canada
by Iris Johansen

bestselling author of THE GOLDEN BARBARIAN

Jon Sandell is a man with many secrets and one remarkable power, the ability to read a woman's mind, to touch her soul, to know her every waking desire. His vital mission is to rescue a woman unaware of the danger she is in. But who will protect her from him?